Acclaim for David Malouf

"Malouf is a master of narrative technique. . . . He is one of our finest writers, a poet with an ear for language."
—*San Francisco Chronicle*

"Malouf's writing [is] rich and dense with meaning and atmosphere. . . . Marvelous prose under tight control."
—*The New York Review of Books*

"A masterfully graceful prose writer."   —*Daily News*

"A storyteller of achievement, for whom simple things gracefully become totems for deeper thought."
—*Philadelphia Inquirer*

"[Malouf is] a writer with great imaginative powers and a gift for acute psychological characterization."
—*Boston Globe*

"Malouf is at once powerful and tender."
—*Los Angeles Times*

ALSO BY David Malouf

David Malouf

Fly Away Peter

David Malouf is the author of, among other works, nine novels, including *The Great World*, which in 1991 won the Commonwealth Writers Prize and the Prix Fémina Étranger. In 1993 *Remembering Babylon* was shortlisted for the Booker Prize and named by *Time* as one of the best works of fiction for that year. It received the *Los Angeles Times* Book Award for Fiction in 1994 and was the winner of the International IMPAC Dublin Literary Award. Malouf divides his time between Australia and Tuscany.

INTERNATIONAL

Fly Away Peter

David Malouf

VINTAGE INTERNATIONAL
Vintage Books
A Division of Random House, Inc.
New York

FIRST VINTAGE INTERNATIONAL EDITION, JUNE 1998

Copyright © 1982 by David Malouf

All rights reserved under International and
Pan-American Copyright Conventions.
Published in the United States by Vintage Books,
a division of Random House, Inc., New York.
Originally published in hardcover in Great Britain by
Chatto & Windus Ltd, London, in 1982.

Poetry excerpt by Wallace Stevens from *Collected Poems*
by Wallace Stevens. Copyright 1954 by Wallace Stevens.
Reprinted by permission of Alfred A. Knopf., Inc.

Library of Congress Cataloging-in-Publication Data
Malouf, David, 1934–
Fly away Peter / David Malouf.
p.   cm.
ISBN 0-679-77670-2
1. World War, 1914–1918—Fiction. I. Title.
PR9619.3.M265F5   1998
823—dc21   98-11054
CIP

Random House Web address: www.randomhouse.com

Printed in the United States of America
10 9 8 7 6 5 4 3 2

For Elizabeth Riddell

Man is an exception, whatever else he is. If it is
not true that a divine creature fell, then we can
only say that one of the animals went entirely off
its head.

G.K. Chesterton

Here is the bread of time to come,

Here is its actual stone. The bread
Will be our bread, the stone will be

Our bed and we shall sleep by night.
We shall forget by day, except

The moment when we choose to play
The imagined pine, the imagined jay.

Wallace Stevens

1

All morning, far over to his left where the light of
the swamp ended and farmlands began, a clumsy
shape had been lifting itself out of an invisible paddock
and making slow circuits of the air, climbing, dipping,
rolling a little, then disappearing below the trees.

The land in that direction rose gradually towards
far, intensely blue mountains that were soft blue at
this time of day but would later approach purple. The
swamp was bordered with tea-trees, some of them
half-standing in water and staining the shallows there
a tobacco brown. Its light was dulled by cloud
shadows, then, as if an unseen hand were rubbing it
with a cloth, it brightened, flared, and the silver shone
through.

A vast population of waterbirds lived in the swamp,
and in the paddocks and wooded country beyond
were lorikeets, rosellas and the different families of
pigeons – fruit-pigeon, bronze-wings, the occasional
topknot or squatter – and high over all stood the birds
of prey, the hawks and kestrels. But the big shadow
was that of a bi-plane that all morning rose and dip-

ped, its canvas drawn tight across struts, all its piano-wires singing. It was a new presence here and it made Jim Saddler uneasy. He watched it out of the corner of his eye and resented its bulk, the lack of purpose in its appearance and disappearance at the tree line, the lack of pattern in its lumbering passes, and the noise it made, which was also a disturbance and new.

Over behind him, where all this swampland drained into the Pacific, were dunes, shifting sand held together with purple-flowering pigweed and silvery scrub; then the surf – miles of it. You could walk for hours beside its hissing white and never see a soul. Just great flocks of gulls, and pied oyster-catchers flitting over the wet light, stopping, starting off again; not at random but after tiny almost transparent crabs, and leaving sharp, three-toed prints.

He had a map of all this clearly in his head, as if in every moment of lying here flat on his belly watching some patch of it for a change of shape or colour that would be a small body betraying itself, he were also seeing it from high up, like the hawk, or that fellow in his flying-machine. He moved always on these two levels, through these two worlds: the flat world of individual grassblades, seen so close up that they blurred, where the ground-feeders darted about striking at worms, and the long view in which all this part of the country was laid out like a relief-map in the Shire Office – surf, beach, swampland, wet paddocks, dry, forested hill-slopes, jagged blue peaks. Each section of it supported its own birdlife; the territorial borders of each kind were laid out there, invisible but clear, which the birds were free to cross but didn't; they stayed for the most part within strict limits. They stayed. Then at last, when the time came, they upped and left; flew off in groups, or in couples or alone, to where they came from and lived in the other part of the year, far out over the earth's rim in the Islands, or in China or Europe.

Holding one of them in the glasses he was aware of that also. *This creature that I could catch so easily in my hands, feeling the heart beat and the strong wings flutter against my palms, has been further and higher even than that clumsy plane. It has been to Siberia. Its tiny quick eye has seen something big. A whole half of the earth.*

The bi-plane appeared again, climbing steeply against the sun. Birds scattered and flew up in all directions. It flopped down among them, so big, so awkward, so noisy. Did they wonder what it ate? A hundred times bigger than any hawk or eagle its appetite would be monstrous. Did they keep their sharp eyes upon it?

Jim's eye was on the swamphen. He had been watching it for nearly an hour with a pair of field-glasses provided by Ashley Crowther. There was a nest on a platform there among the reeds, with maybe five or six creamy-brown eggs.

Ashley Crowther was a young man, not all that much older than himself, who had been away to school in England and then at Cambridge, and had recently come back to manage his father's land. He owned all the land beyond the swamp and from the

3

swamp towards the ocean. The bi-plane was flying out of one of Ashley Crowther's paddocks and was piloted, Jim guessed, by one of Ashley's friends. There were regular weekend-guests at the homestead these days, young fellows, and also ladies, who arrived in automobiles wearing caps or with their heads swathed in voile against the dust of country roads, to ride, to eat big meals in the lamplit house and to dance to gramophone music on the verandah.

The swampland also belonged to Ashley, and because he was interested in the birds he had set Jim to watch it and to record its various comings and goings. It was a new idea that came from Europe, though Queensland in fact had passed a law to protect birds nearly forty years ago, before any other place in the Empire.

Ashley Crowther had sat on a log chewing a grass-stem and looked out dreamily over the swamp, and Jim had recognized right off a man he could talk to, even if they said nothing at all; and had shifted his feet, unused to this, and uncertain where it might lead. It wasn't his place to make an opening.

'Listen,' Ashley had said. With no preliminaries, as if the whole thing had just that moment taken shape in his head, he laid out his plan; and Jim, who till then had been merely drifting, and might have drifted as far as the city and become a mill-hand or a tram-conductor, saw immediately the scope of it and felt his whole life change. A moment before this odd bloke had been a stranger. Now he stuck out his hand to be shaken and there was all the light of the swampland

4

and its swarming life between them, of which Jim was to have sole charge.

He was twenty, and Ashley Crowther was a tall, inarticulate young man of twenty-three, who looked at times as if he was stooping under the weight of his watch-chain and who stumbled not only over words but over his own boots. But he had said 'Well then, you're my man,' having that sort of power, and Jim was made. All the possibilities that for the past two years had tugged and nagged at him – the city, marriage, drink, the prospect of another thirty years of dragging his boot over sawdust in the Anglers' Arms, of sitting reading the sports page with his feet propped on the bed-head while rain dripped into a basin on his bedroom floor, the sullenness and hard-jawed resentment of months that were all Sundays – suddenly hauled off and lifted. He was made free of his own life.

'Jim's a new man,' his father told his drinking mates up at the pub with studied gloom. He had projected for Jim a life as flat, save for the occasional down-turn, as his own. It was inevitable, he declared, 'for the likes of us.'

'What does it mean,' Jim had wanted to ask, 'the likes of us?' Except for the accidental link of blood he saw nothing in common between his father and himself and resented the cowardly acceptance of defeat that made his father feel this change in his fortunes as a personal affront. But he had had enough cuffs from the old man, over lesser issues than this, to have learned that there were some questions that were better not put.

5

'You're a bloody fool,' the old man told him, 'if you trust that lot, with their fancy accents and their new-fangled ideas. And their machines! You'd be better off gettin' a job in Brisbane and be done with it. Better off, y'hear? Better!' And he punched hard into the palm of his hand.

There was in his father a kind of savagery that Jim kept at arm's length; not because he feared to be its victim in the physical sense – he had been often enough and it was nothing much, it was merely physical – but because he didn't want to be infected. It was of a kind that could blast the world. It allowed nothing to exist under its breath without being blackened, torn up by the roots, slashed at, and shown when ripped apart to have a centre as rotten as itself. His father had had a hard life, but that didn't explain it. 'I was sent out to work at ten years old by *my* old man. Put to the plough like a bloody animal. Sent to sleep in straw. All that, all that!' But it didn't account for what the man was. It had happened equally to others in those days; and besides, Jim might have argued, did you treat me any better? No, the baleful look his father turned on the world had no reason, it simply was.

He swallowed his resentment and determined to say no more. As for Ashley Crowther, he would take the risk. Something in the silence that existed between them, when they just sat about on stumps and Ashley crossed his legs and rested his chin in the palm of his hand, made Jim believe there could be common ground between them, whatever the difference. There was in Ashley a quiet respect for things that Jim also respected.

None of this had to be stated. Ashley was too incoherent to have explained and Jim would have been embarrassed to hear it, but he understood. All this water, all these boughs and leaves and little clumps of tussocky grass that were such good nesting-places and feeding grounds belonged inviolably to the birds. The rights that could be granted to a man by the Crown, either for ninety-nine years or in perpetuity, were of another order and didn't quite mean what they said. This strange man with his waistcoat and his watch-chain, his spotted silk tie and Pommie accent, had seen that from the start.

But there was more. There was also, on Ashley's part, a recognition that Jim too had rights here, that these acres might also belong, though in another manner, to him. Such claims were ancient and deep. They lay in Jim's knowledge of every blade of grass and drop of water in the swamp, of every bird's foot that was set down there; in his having a vision of the place and the power to give that vision breath; in his having, most of all, the names for things and in that way possessing them. It went beyond mere convention or the law.

There was something here, Jim thought, that answered his unasked question, 'what does it mean, the likes of us?', by cancelling it out in some larger view, and it was this that he was prepared to trust. The view was Ashley's and it was generous. It made a place for Jim, and left room as well for the coming and going of a thousand varieties, even the most alien, of birds.

2

Ashley Crowther had come home after more than twelve years to find himself less a stranger here than he expected.

He had been at school in England, then at Cambridge, then in Germany for a year studying music, and might have passed anywhere on that side of the world for an English gentleman. He spoke like one; he wore the clothes – he was much addicted to waistcoats and watch-chains, an affectation he might have to give up, he saw, in the new climate; he knew how to handle waiters, porters, commissionaires etc. with just the right mixture of authority, condescension and jolly good humour. He was in all ways cultivated, and his idleness, which is what people here would call it, gave him no qualms. He took a keen interest in social questions, and saw pretty clearly that in the coming years there would be much to be done, stands to be taken, forces to be resisted, changes to be made and come to terms with. The idea excited him. He approved of change. With all that to think of he didn't see that one had also to have a vocation, a job named and paid for

8

and endured for a certain number of hours each day, to be a serious person.

Ashley Crowther was a very serious person. He was dreamy, certainly, and excitably inarticulate, but he liked what was practical, what worked, and in the three years since he came of age had owned four automobiles. Now he was interested in the newest thing of all, the air. He didn't fly himself, but his friend Bert did, and he was quite content, as in other cases, to play the patron and look on.

In the crude categories that had been in operation at Cambridge, athlete or aesthete, he had found himself willy-nilly among the latter. He had never been much good at games – his extreme thinness was against him – and he not only played the piano, Chopin and Brahms, but could whistle all the *Leitmotifs* from *The Ring*. But his childhood had been spent in the open, he had never lost his pleasure in wide spaces and distant horizons, in climbing, riding, going on picnics, and the creatures he had been surrounded by in those early years had never deserted his dreams. Moving as they did in the other half of the world, far under the actualities of the daylight one, they had retained their primitive power and kept him in touch with a continent he had been sent away from at eleven but never quite left. Perhaps that is why when he came back at twenty-three he was not a stranger.

Waking up that first morning in the old house – not in his own room, the room of his childhood, but in the big main bedroom since he was now the master – he had been overwhelmed by the familiarity of things:

the touch of the air on his skin – too warm; the sharpness of the light even at twenty to seven – it might have been noon elsewhere; above all, since it is what came closest to the centre of his being, the great all-embracing sound that rose from the dazzling earth, a layered music, dense but deeply flowing, that was clippered insects rubbing their legs together, birdnotes, grass-stems chaffing and fretting in the breeze. It immediately took him up and carried him back. He stepped out on to the verandah in his pyjamas – no need for even the lightest gown – and it was all about him, the whole scene trembled upon it. The flat earth had been transposed into another form and made accessible to a different sense. An expansive monotone, its excited fluting and throbbing and booming from distended throats had been the ground-bass, he saw, of every music he had ever known. It was the sound his whole being moved to. He stood barefoot on the gritty boards and let it fill his ear.

'How can you do it?' his friends back there had said, commiserating but admiring his courage, which they altogether exaggerated.

'It's my fate,' he had replied.

The phrase pleased him. It sounded solemn and final. But he was glad just the same to discover, now he was here, that he was not a stranger, and to feel, looking out on all this, the contentment of ownership and continuity.

It was his grandfather who had taken up the claim and put his name to the deeds; but he had died while the land was still wild in his head, a notion, no more, of what he had staked out in a strange and foreign continent that his children must make real. Ashley's father had created most of what lay before him. Now it was his.

There was still everything to do – one saw that at a glance. But Ashley saw things differently from his father and grandfather. They had always had in mind a picture they had brought from 'home', orderly fields divided by hedgerows, to which the present landscape, by planning and shaping, might one day be made to approximate. But for Ashley this was the first landscape he had known and he did not impose that other, greener one upon it; it was itself. Coming back, he found he liked its mixture of powdery blues and greens, its ragged edges, its sprawl, the sense it gave of being unfinished and of offering no prospect of being finished. These things spoke of space, and of a time in which nature might be left to go its own way and still yield up what it had to yield; there was that sort of abundance. For all his cultivation, he liked what was unmade here and could, without harm, be left that way.

There was more to Ashley Crowther's image of the world than his formal clothes might have suggested – though he was, in fact, without them at this moment, barefoot on scrubbed boards – or, since he was shy, his formal manners, which were not so easily laid aside.

After breakfast he changed into a cotton shirt, twills, boots and wide-brimmed hat and took a ride round his property, beginning with the little iron fenced enclosure where his parents, his grandparents and several

11

smaller brothers and sisters were interred under sculptured stone.

The Monuments, as they were called, were only visible from the house when the big wheat-paddock was bare, since they stood in the very middle of it. He remembered how, as a child, he had crawled in among the rustling stems to find the place, his lost ancestral city, or had sat on a fence-post while a harvester, moving in wide circles, had gradually revealed it: tall columns standing alone among the flattened grain, already, even in those days, so chipped and stained that they might have been real monuments going back centuries rather than a mere score of years to the first death. He made his way towards them now, through the standing wheat, and sat for a moment with his hat off. Then rode on.

He saw much that day, though nothing like the whole – that would take weeks, months even. In the evening, after bathing and changing, he sat alone on the verandah and decided he would make the house, once again, a place where people came; he couldn't keep all this, or his excitement in it, to himself. The smokiness of the hour, the deepening blue of the hills and all the gathering night sounds, were too good not to share, and he was by nature generous.

Within two months he had done all that. He had visited most places on the property and got a clear view of all its various activities and the men who were in charge or carried them out. When he looked at the manager's books now he saw real faces behind the names, and behind the figures fenced places and wild, and knew what it all meant in hours worked and distance covered. It had found its way down, painfully at first, then pleasurably, into his wiry muscles, in days of riding or walking or sitting about yarning in the sun.

The house too had been given a new life. Weekend guests came and were put up in the big verandah rooms with their cedar wardrobes and tiled washstands and basins. They strolled on the verandah in the early morning, having been drawn out by the brightness of the light, and sat in deep squatters' chairs in the evening to enjoy the dusk, while Ashley, supplementing the music of the landscape itself, played to them on an upright. They ate huge meals under a fan in the dining-room, with a lazy Susan to deal at breakfast with four different sorts of jam and two of honey, one a comb, and at dinner with the sauces and condiments; they took picnics down to the creek. The tennis court was weeded and spread with a reddish-pink hard stuff that was made from smashed anthills, and they played doubles, the ladies in skirts and blouses, the young men in their shirtsleeves. Bert came with his flying-machine. They watched it wobble in over the swamp, then circle the house and touch down, a bit unsteadily, in the home paddock. It sat there in the heat haze like a giant bird or moth while cows flicked their tails among cow-pats, and did not seem out of place. It was a landscape, Ashley thought, that could accommodate a good deal. That was his view of it. It wasn't so clearly defined as England or Germany; new things could enter and find a place there. It might be old, even very old, but it was more open than Europe to what was still to come.

He also discovered Jim.

While he was riding one day in the low scrub along the swamp the young man had simply started up out of the earth at his feet; or rather, had rolled over on his back, where he had been lying in the grass, and then got to his feet cursing. Ashley hadn't seen the other creature that started up yards off and went flapping into a tree. He was too astonished that some fellow should be lying there on his belly in the middle of nowhere, right under the horse's hooves, and felt the oath, though he didn't necessarily attach it to himself, to be on the whole unjustified.

The young man stood, thin-faced, heavy shouldered, in worn moleskins and a collarless shirt, and made no attempt to explain his presence or to acknowledge any difference between Ashley and himself except that one was mounted and the other had his two feet set firmly on the earth. He brushed grass-seed from his trousers with an old hat and stood his ground. Ashley, oddly, found this less offensive than he ought.

'What were you doing?' he asked. It was a frank curiosity he expressed. There was nothing of reproach in it.

'Watchin' that Dollar bird,' Jim told him. 'You scared it off.'

'Dollar bird?'

'Oriental,' Jim said. 'Come down from the Moluccas.'

His voice was husky and the accent broad; he drawled. The facts he gave were unnecessary and might have been pedantic. But when he named the bird, and again when he named the island, he made them sound, Ashley thought, extraordinary. He endowed them with some romantic quality that was really in himself. An odd interest revealed itself, the fire of an individual passion.

Ashley slipped down from the saddle and they stood side by side, the grass almost at thigh level. Jim pointed.

'It's in that ironbark, see?' He screwed up his eyes. 'There, over to the left. Second branch from the top. Red beak. Purple on the throat and tail-feathers. See?'

Ashley stared, focused, found the branch; and then, with a little leap of surprise and excitement, the bird – red beak, purple throat, all as the young man had promised.

'I can see it!' he exclaimed, just like a child, and they both grinned. The young man turned away and sat on a log. He took the makings of a smoke from his pocket. Ashley stumbled forward.

'Have one of mine,' he insisted. 'No, really.' He offered the case, already snapped open, with the gold-tipped tailor-mades under a metal band that worked like a concertina.

'Thanks,' the young man said, his square fingers making an awkward job of working the band. He turned the cylinder, so utterly smooth and symmetrical, in his fingers, looking at the gold paper round the tip, then put it to his lower lip, struck a wax match,

15

which he cupped in his hand against the breeze, and held it out to Ashley, who dipped his head towards it and blew out smoke. Jim lit his own cigarette and flipped the match with his thumbnail. All this action carried them over a moment of nothing-more-to-say into an easy silence. Ashley led his horse to a stump opposite, and crossing his legs, and with his body hunched forward elbow to knee, fell intensely still, then said abruptly:

'Are you out here often? Watching, I mean?'

'Fairly.'

'Why?'

'I dunno. It's something to do, isn' it?' He looked about, his grey eyes narrowed, and the land was a flat circle all round, grass-tips, tree-stumps, brush, all of it seemingly still and silent, all of it crowded and alive with eyes, beaks, wing-tips.

Ashley followed his gaze. The land shifted into a clearer focus, and he might himself have been able, suddenly, to see it in all its detail, the individual eye infinitesimally rolling, the red beak in a spray of gum-flowers, the tiny body at ground level among the roots, one of the seed-eaters, coloured like the earth. He was intensely aware for a moment how much life there might be in any square yard of it. And he owned a thousand acres.

But even if he looked and saw, he would have no name for it. *Dollar bird*. This youth had the names.

'Where did you learn?' he asked, out of where his own thoughts had led him.

'Oh, here 'n there. Some of it from books. Mostly,

16

you know, it's –' Jim found it difficult to explain that it was almost a sense he had, inexplicable even to himself. To have said that might have been to claim too much. A gift. Was it a gift? 'In time,' he said, 'you get to know some things and the rest you guess. If you're any good you guess right. Nine times in a hundred,' and he gave a laugh. Ashley laughed too. He drew himself tighter together, the knotted legs, the elbows in hard against his body, and the laughter was like an imp he had bottled up in there that suddenly came bubbling out.

'Listen,' he said, 'how would you like to work for me? How would you –'

He stopped, breathless with the excitement of it. The landscape, the whole great circle of it, grassheads, scrub, water, sky, quite took his breath away. All those millions of lives as they entering what he had just conceived. 'How would you like,' he said, 'to do all this on a proper basis? I mean, make lists. We could turn this' (it was the notion of time that took his breath away, the years, the decades), 'into an observing place, a sanctuary. It's mine, I can make what I want of it. And you'd be just the man.'

Smoke trailed from Jim's lips in a steady stream. He had been waiting for so long for something like this to present itself, and now this Ashley Crowther fellow comes up behind him on a horse and offers it, just like that – not just a job but work, years, a lifetime.

The young man's silence threw Ashley off balance.

'I'd make it worth your while, of course.' He swallowed. The landscape itself, he thought, ought to add its appeal; for it was an appeal more than an offer he was making, and it was on the land's behalf that it was made. 'How does it strike you, then?' he asked lamely.

Jim nodded. 'It sounds alright.'

'Well then,' Ashley said, laughing and jumping to his feet, 'you're my man.' He thrust his hand out, and both standing now, feet on the ground, at the centre, if they could have seen themselves, of a vast circle of grass and low greyish scrub, with beyond them on one side tea-trees then paddocks, and on the other tea-trees then swamp then surf, in a very formal manner, with Ashley stooping slightly since he was so much the taller, and Jim quite square, they shook on it. It was done.

3

If Ashley discovered Jim, it was Jim who discovered Miss Harcourt, Miss Imogen Harcourt.

He was on his belly again, with a note-pad in his pocket, a stub of pencil behind his ear and the field-glasses Ashley Crowther had provided screwed firmly into his head – they might have been a fixture.

He was watching a sandpiper in a patch of marshy bank, one of the little wood sandpipers that appear each summer and come, most of them, from Northern Asia or Scandanavia, nesting away at the top of the world on the tundras or in the Norwegian snows and making their long way south.

It amazed him, this. That he could be watching, on a warm day in November, with the sun scorching his back, the earth pricking below and the whole land-scape dazzling and shrilling, a creature that only weeks ago had been on the other side of the earth and had found its way here across all the cities of Asia, across lakes, deserts, valleys between high mountain ranges, across oceans without a single guiding mark, to light on just this bank and enter the round frame of his binoculars; completely contained there in its small life – striped breast and sides, white belly, yellow legs, the long beak investigating a pool for food, occasionally lifting its head to make that peculiar three-note whistle – and completely containing, somewhere invisibly within, that blank white world of the northern ice-cap and the knowledge, laid down deep in the tiny brain, of the air-routes and courses that had brought it here. Did it know where it had arrived on the earth's surface? Did it retain, in that small eye, some image of the larger world, so that it could say *There I was so many darknesses ago and now I am here, and will stay a time, and then go back*; seeing clearly the space between the two points, and knowing that the distance, however great, could quite certainly be covered a second time in the opposite direction because the further side was still visible, either there in its head or in the long memory of its kind.

The idea made Jim dizzy. That, or the sun, or the effort of watching. He raised the glasses to rest a moment, and in doing so caught something unexpected that flashed through the frames and was gone.

Where?

He let the glasses travel across, back, up a little, down, making various frames for the landscape, and there it was again: a face under a sun-bonnet. It was lined and brown, and was at the moment intensely fixed upon something, utterly absorbed. He shifted the glasses and found a black box on a tripod. The face ducked down behind it. The composite figure that now filled the frame was of a grey skirt, voluminous

20

and rather bedraggled, topped by the black box wearing a sun-bonnet. The black box was pointing directly towards him. Could it be him that she was photographing?

It was only after a minute that he realized the truth. What the woman had in her sights was the same sandpiper he had been holding, just a few seconds ago, in his binoculars. For some time, without either of them being aware of it, they had, in all this landscape, and among all its creatures, been fixing their attention from different sides on the same spot and on the same small white-breasted body.

He wasn't all that much surprised by the coincidence. It seemed less extraordinary than that this few ounces of feather and bone should have found its way here from Siberia or Norway. That was itself so unlikely that men had preferred to believe, and not so long ago, either, that when the season turned, some birds had simply changed their form as others changed their plumage – that swallows, for example, became toads – and had actually given detailed accounts of the transformation: the birds gathering in such numbers, on reeds, on lake beds, that the stems bent low under their weight, and at the point where the reeds touched the water the swallows were transmuted, drew in their wings and heads, splayed their beaks to a toad-mouth, lowered their shrill cries to a throaty creaking, and went under the surface till it was time for them to be re-born overnight in their old shapes in twittering millions.

Meanwhile the tripod had transformed itself back

into a woman. She was stomping about in her grey skirt; an old girl, he guessed, of more than fifty, with grey curls under the bonnet and boots under the skirt. She lifted the tripod, snapped it shut, set it over her shoulder, and moved off with the rest of her equipment into the scrub.

Later, at the Anglers' Arms, he discovered her name and went down river to the weatherboard cottage she had bought and introduced himself.

The house was in bad shape. Sheets of iron were lifting from the roof, making the whole thing look as if it had grown wings and were about to rise out of this patch of scrub and settle in another on the far side of the hill. The weatherboard was grey, there were gaps in the verandah rails, and one window that had lost its glass was stuffed with yellowish newspaper. Stumps of what might once have been a paling fence stuck up here and there in a wilderness of briars, and beyond them, in the yard, a lemon tree had gone back to the wild state, with big lumpy fruit among inch-long thorns. On one side of the concrete step to the verandah was a washing tub, all pitted and crumbling with rust. It contained a skeletal fern. On the other two kerosene tins packed with dry earth put forth miraculous carnations, pink and white.

'Anyone home?' he called.

There was a voice from somewhere within, but so far off that it seemed to be replying from the depths of a house several times larger than this one, a deep hallway leading to cool, richly furnished rooms.

'Who is it?' An English voice.

'Me,' he replied foolishly, as a child would; then added in a deeper voice, 'Jim Saddler. I work for Mr Crowther.'

'Come on in,' the voice invited, 'I'll be with you in just a moment. I'm in the dark room.'

He stepped across a broken board, pushed the door and went in. It was clean enough, the kitchen, but bare: a scrubbed table and one chair, cups on hooks, a wood stove in a corrugated iron alcove. Wood-chunks, newspapers, a coloured calender.

'I can't come for a bit,' the voice called. 'Take a seat.'

The voice, he thought, might not have belonged to the woman he had seen out there in the swamp. It sounded younger, like that of someone who keeps up a running conversation while sitting in close conference with a chip-heater and six inches of soapy water; the voice of a woman engaged on something private, intimate, who lets you just close enough, with talk, to feel uncomfortable about what you cannot see. He didn't have much idea what happened in dark-rooms; photography was a mystery.

He examined the calendar. Pictures of English countryside. Turning the leaves back to January, then forward again through the year. Minutes passed.

'There!' she said, and came out pinning a little gold watch to the tucked bodice of her blouse. She was a big, round-faced woman, and the grey curls now that he saw them without the bonnet looked woollen, they might have been a wig.

'Jim Saddler,' he said again, rising.

She offered her hand, which was still damp where

she had just dried it, and they shook. Her handshake, he thought, was firmer than his. At least, it was to begin with.

'Imogen Harcourt. Would you like tea?'

'Thanks,' he said, 'if it's no trouble.'

He wondered about the one chair.

'I've come about that sandpiper,' he said straight out. 'I seen you taking a picture of it.'

'Did you?'

'Yes I did. I work for Ashley Crowther, *Mister* Crowther, I'm his bird man. I keep lists –.' He was shy of making too much of it and made too little. He could never bring himself to say the word that might have properly explained.

'I know,' she admitted, swinging back to face him with the filled kettle in her hand. 'I've seen you. I saw you yesterday.'

'Did you?' he said foolishly, not being used to that; to being *seen*. 'Well then,' he said, 'we're more or less on terms.'

She laughed. 'More or less. Do you take milk?'

She couldn't tell for the moment whether they would be friends or not; whether he had come here to share something or to protect a right. He was awkward, he had dignities. His pale hair stuck out straw-like where it was unevenly but closely cropped, and he stood too much at attention, as if defending narrow ground.

Jim too was puzzled. It was mostly younger women who spoke straight up at you like that, out of the centre of their own lives. Pretty women. Wives, mothers, unmarried aunts had generally settled more comfortably into the conventions than Miss Imogen Harcourt had; they tried harder to please. Though she wasn't what his father would have called a character. She was independent but not odd.

They drank their tea. There was, after all, no trouble about the chair. She half-sat, half-leaned on the window-ledge, and told him at once, without prompting, what there was to tell of her story. She had come here from Norfolk, six years ago, with a brother who'd had a mind to try gold-mining and gone to Mount Morgan but had failed to make a fortune and gone home again. She had decided to stay. She offered no explanation of that. What her intention had been in first following her brother to the other side of the world and then failing to follow him home again was not revealed. She had a small income and was supplementing it by taking nature photographs for a London magazine.

'Birds,' Jim specified.

'Not always. But yes, often enough. That sandpiper took my fancy because it was one of my favourites at home – they come down from the north, you know, and winter among us. In Norfolk, I mean.'

'And here.'

'Yes, here too. It's odd, isn't it? To come halfway across the world and find –. It made me feel homesick. So I set up quickly, got a good shot, and there it is. Homesickness dealt with. Stuffed into the box.'

He found he understood almost everything she said straight off, and this was unusual.

'Could I see it? The photo?'

'Why not?'

She led him into the hallway, past what must have been a bedroom, and into the darkness at the end of the hall.

It was the best room in the house; orderly, well set-up, with two sinks, a lamp, black cloth to cover the windows. He understood that too. When he stepped into the place it wasn't just the narrowness of the space they stood in, among all the apparatus of a hobby, or trade, that made him feel they had moved closer. He saw, because she allowed him to see, a whole stretch of her life, wider, even here in a dark-room, than anything he could have guessed from what she had already told – Norfolk, her brother, the tent city at Mount Morgan. He liked the order, the professionalism, the grasp all this special equipment suggested of a competence. There were racks for her plates, bottles of chemicals all neatly labelled, rubber gloves, a smell of something more than lavender.

'So this is it,' he said admiringly as he might have spoken to any man. 'Where you work.'

'Yes,' she said, 'here and out there.'

[As he was to discover, she often made these distinctions, putting things clearer, moving them into a sharper focus.

'The light, and then the dark.']

She took a sheet of paper and offered it to him, and looked anxious as he subjected it to scrutiny.

It was the sandpiper. Perfect. Every speckle, every stripe on the side where it faded off into the white of

26

the underbelly, the keen eye in the lifted head – he felt oddly moved to see the same bird in this other dimension. Moved too at the trouble it must have taken, and the quick choices, to get just that stance, which was so perfectly characteristic; her own keen eye measuring the bird's and discovering the creature's taut, spring-like alertness. Did she know so much about birds? Or did some intuition guide her? *This is it; this is the moment when we see into the creature's unique life.* That too might be a gift.

The sandpiper was in sharp focus against a blur of earth and grass-stems, as if two sets of binoculars had been brought to bear on the same spot, and he knew that if the second pair could now be shifted so that the landscape came up as clear as the bird, he too might be visible, lying there with a pair of glasses screwed into his head. He was there but invisible; only he and Miss Harcourt might ever know that he too had been in the frame, hidden among those soft rods of light that were grass-stems and the softer sunbursts that were grass-heads or tiny flowers. To the unenlightened eye there was just the central image of the sandpiper with its head attentively cocked. And that was as it should be. It was the sandpiper's picture.

'Perfect,' he breathed.

'Yes,' she said, 'I was pleased too.'

They looked at the bird between them, having moved quickly, since yesterday, to where they now stood with just this sheet of paper between them on which the bird's passage through its own brief huddle of heat and energy had been caught for a moment and fixed, maybe for ever.

'I must show this,' Jim said, 'to Ashley Crowther.'

So they became partners, all three, and a week later Jim told her of the sanctuary, actually using the word out loud for the first time, since he was certain now that there was nothing in her that would scoff at the grandness of it, but blushing just the same; the blood rose right up into the lobes of his ears.

He never uttered the word again. He didn't have to. When he talked to Miss Harcourt, as when he talked to Ashley Crowther, they spoke only of 'the birds'.

4

Sometimes, when Ashley Crowther had a party of friends down for the weekend, or for the Beaudesert races, Jim would take them out in a flat-bottomed boat, and for an hour or two they would drift between dead white trees over brackish water, its depths the colour of brewed tea, its surface a layer of drowned pollen inches thick in places, a burnished gold. Parting the scum, they would break in among clouds.

Ashley would be in the bow, his knees drawn up hard under his chin, his arms, in shirt-sleeves, propped upon them, like some sort of effigy, Jim thought – an image of whatever god it was that had charge of this place, a waterbird transmuted. The women, and the young men in blazers who shared the centre of the boat with their provisions, a wicker basket, its silver hasp engraved with the name of the house, would be subdued, tense, held on a breath; held on Jim's breath.

'That,' he would whisper, lifting the pole and letting them slide forward in the stillness, 'is the Sacred Kingfisher. From Borneo.'

The name, in Jim's hushed annunciation of it,

[immediately wrapped the bird in mystery, beyond even the brilliance of its colouring and the strange light the place touched it with.]

'And over there – see? – those are lotus birds. See? Far over. Aw, now they've seen us, they're off. They've got a nest at the edge there, right down at water level. See their feet? Long they are. That's for walking on the lotus leaves, or on waterlily pads, so they don't sink.'

He would push his pole into mud again, putting his shoulder into it and watching the birds flock away, and they would ride smoothly in under the boughs. Nobody spoke. It was odd the way the place imposed itself and held them. Even Ashley Crowther, who preferred music, was silent here and didn't fidget. He sat spell-bound. *And maybe*, Jim thought, *this is music too, this sort of silence*.

What he could not know was to how great a degree these trips into the swamp, in something very like a punt, were for Ashley recreations of long, still afternoons on the Cam, but translated here not only to another hemisphere, but back, far back, into some pre-classical, pre-historic, primaeval and haunted world (it was this that accounted for his mood of suspended wonder) in which the birds Jim pointed out, and might almost have been calling up as he named them in a whisper out of the mists before creation, were extravagantly disguised spirits of another order of existence, and the trip itself – despite the picnic hamper and the champagne bottles laid in ice, and the girls, one of whom was the girl he was about to marry – a water journey in another, deeper sense; which is why he occasionally shivered, and might, looking back, have seen Jim, where he leaned on the pole, straining, a slight crease in his brow and his teeth biting into his lower lip, as the ordinary embodiment of a figure already glimpsed in childhood and given a name in mythology, and only now made real.

'There,' Jim breathed, 'white ibis. They're common enough really. Beautiful, but.' He lifted his eyes in admiration, and at the end of the sentence, his voice as well, to follow their slow flight as they beat away. They might have been swimming, stroke on stroke, through the heavy air. 'And that's a stilt, see? See its blue back? It's a real beauty!'

They would be stilled in the boat, all wonder, who at other times were inclined to giggle, the girls, and worry about their hair or the sit of their clothes, and the young men to stretch their legs and yawn. They were so graceful, these creatures, turning their slow heads as the boat glided past and doubled where the water was clear: marsh terns, spotted crake, spur-winged plover, Lewin water rails. And Jim's voice also held them with its low excitement. He was awkward and rough-looking till they got into the boat. Then he too was light, delicately balanced, and when it was a question of the birds, he could be poetic. They looked at him in a new light and with a respect he wouldn't otherwise have been able to command.

As for Ashley, he liked to show them off: his birds. Or rather, he liked to have Jim show them off, and was pleased at dinner afterwards when his guests praised the ibis, the Sacred Kingfisher, the water rail, as if he had been very clever indeed in deciding that this is what he should collect rather than Meissen figures or Oriental mats.

But in the boat, in the place where the creatures were at home, they passed out of his possession as strangely as they had passed into it, and he might have been afraid then of his temerity in making a claim; they moved with their little lives, if they moved at all, so transiently across his lands – even when they were natives and spent their whole lives there – and knew nothing of Ashley Crowther. They shocked him each time he came here with the otherness of their being. He could never quite accept that they were, he and these creatures, of the same world. It was as if he had inherited a piece of the next world, or some previous one. That was why he felt such awe when Jim so confidently offered himself as an intermediary and named them: 'Look, the Sacred Kingfisher. From Borneo.'

When they stopped to picnic there was talk at last. They came back to reality.

'The nightingale,' a Mrs McNamara informed them, 'that's the most beautiful of all songbirds now.'

'I've never heard it,' a younger woman regretted.

'Oh it's beautiful,' Mrs McNamara assured her. 'But you have to go to Europe. Alas, my love, it was the nightingale.'

'When I was in London,' one of the gentleman told, 'I went to a party in a big house at Twickenham. It was the dead of winter and all night there was a night-ingale twittering away in one of the trees in the garden. I'd never heard anything like it. It was amazing. All the guests went out in troops to listen, it was such a wonder. Only later I found out it was a lark – I mean, some bird-imitator from the music-halls had been hired to sit up there and do it, all rugged up against the cold, poor chap, and blowing on his fingers when he wasn't being a nightingale. It's a wonder he didn't freeze.'

Europe, Jim decided, must be a mad place. And now they said there was to be a war.

He sat apart with his back to a tree and ate the sandwiches he had brought while the others had their spread. Ashley carried a glass of champagne across to him and sat for a bit, with his own glass, but they didn't speak.

Later, when he handed the ladies down on to the wooden landing stage he had constructed, at the end of a twenty-foot cat-walk, each of them said 'Thank you Jim,' and the gentlemen tipped him. Ashley never said thank you, and he pretended not to see the coins that passed, though he wouldn't have deprived Jim of the extra shillings by forbidding it.

Ashley didn't have to thank him. And not at all because Jim was only doing what he was employed to do.

At either end of the boat they held a balance. That was so clear there was no need to state it. There was no need in fact to make any statement at all. But when Ashley wanted someone to talk to, he would come down to where Jim was making a raft of reeds to attract whistlers, or laying out seed, and talk six to the dozen, and in such an incomprehensible rush of syllables that Jim, often, could make neither head nor tail of it, though he didn't mind. Ashley too was an enthusiast, but not a quiet one. Jim understood that, even if he never did grasp what Wagner was – something musical, though not of his sort; and when Ashley gave up words altogether and came to whistling, he was glad to be relieved at last of even pretending to follow. Ashley's talk was one kind of music and the tuneless whistling another. What Ashley was doing, Jim saw, was expressing something essential to himself, like the 'sweet pretty creature' of the willy wagtails (which didn't mean that either). Having accepted the one he could easily accept the other.

Ashley did not present a mystery to Jim, though he did not comprehend him. They were alike and different, that's all, and never so close as when Ashley, watching, chattered away, whistled, chattered again, and then just sat, easily contained in their double silence.

5

The war did come, in mid-August, but quietly, the echo of a shot that had been fired months back and had taken all this time to come round the world and reach them.

Jim happened to be in Brisbane to buy developing paper and dry plates for Miss Harcourt and new boots for himself. By mid-afternoon the news had passed from mouth to mouth all over the city and newsboys were soon crying it at street corners. War! War! It was already several days old, over there, in countries to which they were not linked, and now it had come here.

Some people seemed elated, others stunned. The man at the photography shop, who was some sort of foreigner with a drooping moustache and a bald skull and side-tufts, shook his head as he prepared Jim's parcel. 'A bad business,' he said, 'a catastrophe. Madness!'

Maybe, Jim thought, he had relatives there who would be involved.

'I'm a Swede,' the man told him, Jim didn't know

35

why. He had never said anything like that before.

But others were filled with excitement.

'Imagine,' a girl with very bright eyes said to him at the saddlers where he got his boots. 'I reckon you'll be joining up.'

'Why?' he asked in a last moment of innocence. It hadn't even occurred to him.

The girl's eyes hardened. 'Well I would,' she said fiercely, 'if I was a man. I'd want to be in it. It's an opportunity.' She spoke passionately, bitterly even, but whether at his inadequacy or her own he couldn't tell.

When he stepped out of the shop with his new boots creaking and the old ones in a box under his arm he saw that the streets were, in fact, filled with an odd electricity, as if, while he was inside, a quick storm had come up and equally swiftly passed, changing the sky and setting the pavements, the window-panes, the flanks of passing vehicles in a new and more vivid light. They might have entered a different day, and he wondered if there really had been a change of weather or he only saw the change now because that girl had planted some seed of excitement in him whose sudden blooming here in the open air cast its own reflection on things. He felt panicky. It was as if the ground before him, that had only minutes ago stretched away to a clear future, had suddenly tilted in the direction of Europe, in the direction of *events*, and they were all now on a dangerous slope. That was the impression people gave him. That they were sliding. There was, in all this excitement, an alarming sense that they

36

might be at the beginning of a stampede.

He went into the Lands Office Hotel for a quiet beer; it was where he usually went; it was the least rowdy of the Brisbane pubs.

He found it full of youths who would normally have been at work at this hour in government offices or insurance buildings or shops. They were shouting one another rounds, swaggering a little, swapping boasts, already a solid company or platoon, with a boldness that came from their suddenly being many; and all with their arms around one another's shoulders, hanging on against the slope.

When he went into the back for a piss, one of them, one of the loudest, was leaning with his head on his arm above the tiled wall of the urinal, his body at a forward angle. He seemed to have been like that for a long time.

'Are you alright?' Jim enquired.

'Yes, mate, I'm alright,' the youth said mildly. He tilted himself upright, buttoned up and staggered away. Outside Jim saw him arguing with another fellow, his face very fierce, his fist hammering the other fellow in the upper arm with short hard jabs, the other laughing and pushing him off.

Later, round at the Criterion, it was the same. These were fellows from the law-courts, clerks mostly, wearing three-piece suits, but also noisy. Jim took one look and slipped into the ladies' lounge with its velvet drapes and mirrors, its big glossy-leafed plants in jardinières. He had never dared before. All this excitement had made him bold, but given him at the same time a wish for something softer than the assertions and oaths of the public bar. He met a girl – a woman really – with buttoned boots and a red blouse.

'Are you joining up too?' she asked.

'I dunno,' he lied.

She summed him up quickly. 'From the country?'

'No,' he said, 'the coast.'

'Oh,' she said, but didn't see the difference.

They got talking, and on the assumption that he too was off to the other side of the world and would need something to remember before he went, she invited him to go home with her. He wasn't surprised, he had known all along that this was where their conversation would lead. She was a warm, sandy-headed girl with a sense of humour, inclined to jolly her young men along. She looked at him quizzically and didn't quite understand, but was used to that; young fellows were so different, and so much the same. She touched his hand.

'It's alright. I won't bite, you know.'

He finished his drink slowly, he wasn't in a hurry; feeling quite steady and sure of himself, even on this new ground. Perhaps it was an alternative.

'Right then,' he said, and she gave a wide smile.

Outside the lights were on and there were crowds. Walking up Queen Street they found that in the windows of some of the bigger shops, the department stores where your cash flew about overhead in metal capsules, there were pictures of the King and Queen with crossed flags on either side, one Australian, the other the Union Jack. And the streets did feel different. As if they had finally come into the real world at last, or caught up, after so long, with their own century.

Taking a short tram-ride over the bridge, they walked past palm-trees and Moreton Bay figs till they came to a park, and then, among a row of weatherboard houses, to a big rooming-house with a latticework verandah. He waited on the step while the girl plunged into her leather handbag after the key, and his eye was led, among the huge trunks of the Moreton Bay figs down in the park, to a scatter of glowing points that could have been fireflies, but were, of course, cigarettes. There was some sort of gathering. Suddenly, before the girl could turn her key in the lock, the stillness was broken by a vicious burst of sound, a woman shrieking, then the curses of more than one man.

'Oh,' she said, surprised that he should have stopped and turned, 'abos!' Then repeated it as if he hadn't understood. 'Abos!'

There was an explosion. Breaking glass. A bottle had been dashed against a tree-trunk, and a figure staggered out into the glow of the streetlamp, a black silhouette that became a white-shirted man with his hands over his face and blood between them. He weaved about, but very lightly. He might have been executing a graceful dance, all on his own there, till another figure, hurling itself from the shadows, brought him down. There were thumps. A woman's raucous laughter.

'Abos,' the girl said again with cool disgust, as if the

rituals being enacted, however violent, and in whatever degenerate form, were ordinary and not to be taken note of. 'Aren't you coming in then? Slowcoach!'

Her name was Connie. Jim was quite pleased with himself, and with her as well. Walking back afterwards, in the early evening, with the town very lively still and a lot of young fellows standing about drunk under lampposts, some of them with girls but always talking excitedly to one another, he was able to take all this *action* more easily. Maybe it concerned him, maybe it didn't. So much of what a man was existed within and was known only to himself, and to those, even strangers, to whom he might occasionally, slowly, reveal it.

He stood at the entrance to the bridge and watched the dark waters of the river swarming with lights and saw the butt of his cigarette, glowing all the way, make a wide arc towards it. Nothing had changed.

But back at the boarding house where he usually stayed, he was wakened not long after he fell asleep by a great noise in the street below, and going with one or two others to the balcony, saw a procession making its way towards them of what looked like thousands. He had never seen so many people in one place before. They were young men mostly, and some were in uniform, a group of naval ensigns; but there were also women of all ages, and they were all shouting and cheering and offering up snatches of song. At the head of the crowd, on the shoulders of one of the white-suited navy boys was a little fair-headed lad in a kilt,

40

who was waving his arms about among the flags. He seemed significant in some way – the crowd had chosen him as a symbol – and Jim felt disturbed; he couldn't have said why. Maybe it was the hour. The loose excitement that had been about all day, and had found no focus, had gathered itself to a head at last and was careering through the streets, sweeping everything before it. Sleepy Brisbane! It might be Paris or somewhere, with all these people surging about in the middle of the night, marching with linked arms and chanting slogans. Crowds made him nervous. *Is this what it will be like from now on?* he asked himself. *Will I get used to it?*

One of the old-timers who shared the room with him explained. They were coming, this great press of people, from the Market square, where they had gathered to hear an address from the Lord Mayor. Those noisy outriders of the procession, blatant youths waving scraps of paper, were those who had been enrolled earlier in the evening at the Town Hall, over five hundred they said, and considered themselves to be soldiers already and therefore released from civilian restraint. They were at war.

Jim looked, and wondered if his certainty of a little earlier, that he need not be concerned, would hold. When he went back to bed he couldn't sleep. Far off, the crowd was still spasmodically sending up faint hurrahs, and scraps of tunes, half-familiar, came to his ear: *The Boys of the Old Brigade* – they liked that one, they sang it twice – and more solemnly, *God Save the King*. Lying back with his arms folded under his head, an ordinary if unpatriotic stance, he could imagine all those others falling still and coming to attention as they sang. It might, after all, be serious.

In the morning, as he buttoned his shirt at the window, he looked again at the street where the procession had passed – it was littered with tramtickets and sheets of trampled newspaper that sailed in the westerly – then across the flat, weatherboard city to the hills. By midday he was home.

'Anything much going on in Brisbane?' Miss Harcourt enquired.

'Well,' Jim said, 'you know. The war. Not much otherwise.'

Miss Harcourt looked concerned for a moment and he thought she too might ask if he would go. But she didn't.

Jim stroked his upper lip, where for two days now he had been nursing the beginning of a moustache.

6

They were the days of the big migrations, those last days of August and early September, and Jim spent long hours observing and noting down new arrivals: the first *refugees* Miss Harcourt called them – a strange word, he wondered where she had heard it. He never had.

Tree martins first, but they came only from the Islands and they came to breed; great flocks of them were suddenly there overnight, already engaged in re-making old nests; dotterel and grey-crowned knots, the various tattlers; once a lone greenshank; then sharp-tailed sandpipers, wood sandpipers from the Balkans, whimbrel, grey plover, the Eastern Curlew, Japanese snipe, fork-tailed swifts from Siberia; then much later, towards the turn of the year, Terek sandpipers and pratincoles, the foreign ones in the same flock with locals but clearly distinguishable. He filled book after book with his sightings, carefully noting the numbers and dates of arrival.

The first sight of a bird, there again, after so many months' absence, in the clear round of his glasses, with a bit of local landscape behind it, a grass tuft or reeds or a raft of sticks – that was the small excitement. Quickly he took from his pocket the folded notebook with its red oilcloth cover and the pencil stub from behind his ear, and with his eye still on the bird, made his illegible scribbles. The greater excitement was in inscribing what he had seen into The Book.

Using his best copybook hand, including all the swirls and hooks and tails on the capital letters that you left off when you were simply jotting things down, he entered them up, four or five to a page. This sort of writing was serious. It was giving the creature, through its name, a permanent place in the world, as Miss Harcourt did through pictures. The names were magical. They had behind them, each one, in a way that still seemed mysterious to him, as it had when he first learned to say them over in his head, both the real bird he had sighted, with its peculiar markings and its individual cry, and the species with all its characteristics of diet, habits, preference for this or that habitat, kind of nest, number of eggs etc. Out of air and water they passed through their name, and his hand as he carefully formed its letters, into The Book. Making a place for them there was giving them existence in another form, recognizing their place in the landscape, or his stretch of it: providing 'sanctuary'.

He did his entering up at a particular time and in a particular frame of mind. He liked to have the lamp set just so, and chose a good pen and the best ink; bringing to the occasion his fullest attention; concentrating, as he had on those long boring afternoons at the one teacher school when he had first, rather reluctantly and without at all knowing what it was to be for, learned to form the round, full-bodied letters; and adding with a flourish now the crosses of the big F's, the curled tails of the Q's. He was proud of his work, and pleased when, each week, he was able to show Ashley what he had added.

'Beautiful!' Ashley said for the names, the writing, as he never did for the actual birds, to which he brought only his silence. And that was right. It pleased Jim to have the verbal praise for The Book and silence in the face of the real creature as it lifted its perfect weight from water into air, since in that way Ashley's reaction mirrored his own.

When Ashley and Julia Bell were married at the end of the year Jim presented them with the first of the Books; not exactly as a wedding gift, since that would have been presumptuous, and anyway, the Book was Ashley's already, but as a mark of the occasion. With it went the first of Miss Harcourt's pictures.

7

It was just before that, in late November, that Jim caught one day, in a casual sweep of his glasses over a marshy bank, a creature that he recognized and then didn't: the beak was too long and down-curved, the body too large for any of the various sandpipers. He stared and didn't know what it was. He couldn't have been more puzzled, more astonished, if he'd found a unicorn.

Next day, just on the offchance, he took Miss Harcourt to the place and they waited, silent for the most part, and talking about nothing much when they did talk, while Jim covered the area with his glasses.

Miss Harcourt rather sprawled, with her boots at the end of outstretched legs and her great skirt rumpled, not at all minding the dust. Her bonnet was always lopsided and she didn't mind that either. She had her own rules and kept them but she didn't care for other people's. Jim's father thought her mad: 'That old girl you hang about with,' he sneered 'she's a bit of a hatter.' But she spoke like a lady, she didn't hit the bottle and had, except for her passion for photography

and the equipment she lugged about, no visible eccen-
tricities. People found her, as a subject for gossip,
unmanageable, unrewarding, and she oughtn't to
have been; they resented it. So his father and some
others called her mad but could not furnish evidence.
She refused to become a character. In the end they left
her alone.

Jim chewed a match, working it round and round
his jaw.

At last it was there. It had stepped right out of cover
into a break between reeds. Raising a finger to warn
her, he passed the field-glasses.

'By that clump of reeds,' he whispered, 'at ten
o'clock.'

She took the glasses, drew herself up with some
difficulty, and looked. She gave a little gasp that filled
out and became a sigh, a soft 'Ooooh'.

'What is it?'

She sat back and lowered the glasses to her lap.

'Jim,' she said, 'it's a dunlin. You couldn't miss it.
They used to come in thousands back home, all along
the shore and in the marshes. Common as starlings.'

He took the glasses and stared at this rare creature
he had never laid eyes on till yesterday that was as
common as a starling.

'Dunlin,' he said.

And immediately on his lips it sounded different,
and it wasn't just the vowel. She could have laughed
outright at the newness of the old word now that it had
arrived on this side of the globe, at its difference in his
mouth and hers.

'But *here*,' he said.

He raised the glasses again.

'It doesn't occur.'

But it was there just the same, moving easily about and quite unconscious that it had broken some barrier that might have been laid down a million years ago, in the Pleiocene, when the ice came and the birds found ways out and since then had kept to the same ways. Only this bird hadn't.

'Where does it come from?'

'Sweden. The Baltic. Iceland. Looks like another refugee.'

He knew the word now. Just a few months after he first heard it, it was common, you saw it in the papers every day.

'Tomorrow,' he said, 'we should try and get a photograph. Imagine if it's the very first.' He longed to observe the squat body in flight, to see the wing-formation and the colour of the underwings and the method of it, which had brought the creature, alone of its kind, so far out of the way. But he didn't want it to move. Not till they'd got the photo. He kept the bird in his glasses, as if he could hold it there, on that patch of home ground, so long as he was still looking, the frame of the lens being also in some way magical, a boundary it would find it difficult to cross. He was sweating with the effort, drawing sharp breaths. At last, after a long time, he didn't know how long, he laid the glasses regretfully aside and found Miss Harcourt regarding him with a smile.

'What's the matter?' he said self-consciously, aware

that his intensity sometimes made him a fool.

'Nothing, Jim. Nothing's the matter.'

She had been watching him as closely as he had watched the bird.

Next day she came with her equipment, her 'instruments of martyrdom' she called them, and took the photograph. It wasn't difficult. Jim sat, when it was developed, and stared. It seemed odd to her that it should be so extraordinary, though it was of course, this common little visitor to the shores of her childhood, with its grating cry that in summers back there she would, before it was gone, grow weary of, which here was so exotic, and to him so precious. The way he was clutching the picture! She was amazed by this new vision of him, his determination, his intensity.

'I was the first to see it,' he told her, 'I must be, or someone would have left a record. Miss Harcourt, we've discovered something!'

Rediscovered, she might have said, speaking for her own experience; but was moved just the same to be included.

The most ordinary thing in the world.

She had come so far to where everything was reversed that even that didn't surprise her.

8

One day Bert, Ashley Crowther's aviator friend, offered to take Jim up for a 'spin'.

Jim hesitated, but recognizing that it was really Ashley's doing, and had been intended as a gift, he felt he couldn't refuse, though he had no real curiosity about how things would look from above. New views of things didn't interest him, and he realized, now that it was about to happen, that he had a blood fear, a bone fear, of leaving the earth, some sense, narrow and primitive, derived maybe from a nightmare he had forgotten but not outgrown, that the earth was man's sphere and the air was for the birds, and that though man might break out of whatever bounds had been set him, and in doing so win a kind of glory, it was none the less a stepping out of himself that would lead to no good. Jim was conservative. He preferred to move at ground level. When he raised his eyes skyward it was to wonder at creatures who were other than himself.

But he appeared at the appointed time in the big paddock beyond the house, with his hands in his pockets, his jaw set, and his hat pulled down hard on his brow.

50

The flying machine sat among cow-pats casting a squat shadow. It had two planes mounted one above the other and four booms leading out to the tail, which was a box affair with rudders. The place where you sat (there was room for two sitting in tandem) was on the main plane, and the whole thing, as if no one had considered at the beginning how to hold all the various bits of it together, was crossed and criss-crossed with piano-wire. It looked improvised, as if Bert had put it together especially for the occasion. Jim saw nothing in it that suggested flight, no attempt to reproduce in wood, canvas, metal, the beauty of the bird. It looked more like a monstrous cage, and he wasn't at all surprised to hear Bert refer to it as 'the crate'.

Jim regarded it in a spirit of superstitious dread; and in fact these machines too, in the last months, had entered a new dimension. After just a few seasons of gliding over the hills casting unusual shadows and occasionally clipping the tops of trees, new toys of a boyish but innocent adventuring, they had changed their nature and become weapons. Already they were being used to drop bombs and had been organized, in Europe, into a new fighting arm. Bert was shortly to join such a force. In a week or two he would be sailing to England and soon afterwards might be flying over France. In the meantime they were in Ashley Crowther's dry paddock on a hot day towards the end of June. The air glittered and was still.

'Right you are Jim,' Bert said briskly. He was wearing goggles set far back on his head, which was

51

covered with a leather skull-cap. He looked, Jim thought, with the round eyes set above his forehead, like some sort of cross between a man and a grasshopper. 'Just put these on, old fellow,' he said, offering Jim, with all the jolly camaraderie of a new mystery with its own jargon, and its own paraphernalia, the chance of a similar transformation, 'it's a bit breezy up there, and you'll want to see what there is to see, won't you? That's the whole point. Let me show you how to get in.'

Jim accepted the uniform, but felt too heavy for flight, as if he belonged to an earlier version of the species that would never make the crossing. Conscious of the weight of his boots, his hands, the bones in his pelvis, he climbed in behind Bert, terribly cramped in the narrow seat and already sweating. The breeze was singing in the wires, and it seemed to him for a moment that they were about to make their ascent in some sort of harp that they were taking up, for Ashley's amusement, to be played by the wind. *I know what fascinates Ashley*, he thought. *It's all this piano wire!*

'Good luck!' Ashley shouted, flapping his arms as if he might be about to take off under his own steam.

'Just relax,' Bert shouted. 'The machine does the flying. All we have to do is sit still. You're safe as houses in a crate like this.'

One of the boys from the sheds, who had been coming out to do this all year, gave the propellor a hard spin, the engine turned over, and they began to wobble forward over the coarse grass, gathered speed, ran the length of the paddock, and lifted gently at the last moment over a slip-rail fence, just failing, further on, to touch the top of a windbreak of ragged pines. They were up.

They made a great circuit of the local country, at one point crossing the border. They flew close up to the slopes of the Great Divide, saw a scatter of bright lakes to the south and big rivers down there, high to the point of flooding, rolling brown between cane fields, then turned, and there was the coast: white sand with an edge of lacy surf, then whitecaps in lines behind it, then limitless blue. Bert pointed out a racetrack, and at Southport there was the ferry-crossing and the pier, beyond it the Broadwater dotted with sails and the rip below Stradbroke Island. On the way back, flying lower, Jim had a clear view of what he had already seen in imagination: the swamp and its fringe of tea-tree forest; the paddocks, first green with underlying water then dry and scrubby, that sloped towards the jagged hills, and on the other side the dunes; the two forested hummocks that were Big and Little Burleigh; and a creek entering the sea over a sandbar, through channels of every depth of blue. It was all familiar. He had covered every inch of this country at ground level and had in his mind's eye a kind of map that was not very different from what now presented itself to the physical one. It was, if anything, confirmation; that what he had in his head was a true picture and that he need never go up again.

Once he realized this, and had passed his own test, he could relax and enjoy the sensation of just being there. It was exciting. Especially the rush of air.

But what came to him most clearly was how the map in his own head, which he had tested and found accurate, might be related to the one the birds carried in theirs, which allowed them to find their way – by landmarks, was it? – halfway across the world. It was the wonder of that, rather than the achievement of men in learning how to precipitate themselves into the air at sixty miles an hour, that he brought away from the occasion. And the heads so small!

So it did give him a new view after all.

'I believe you been up in one a' them machines,' his father taunted. 'I don't s'pose you seen any white feathers flyin' about up there. If you did I'd ask you where you reckon they might'v come from. An' I wasn't thinkin' v' angels. Nor Mrs 'Arvey's chooks neither.'

It was a time immediately after news had come of the landings at Gallipoli and the slaughter of the following weeks. People's attitude to the war was changing. Even his father, who hadn't been concerned at first, was suddenly fiercely patriotic and keen for battle. A new seriousness had entered their lives, which was measured by the numbers of the dead they suddenly knew, the fact that history was being made and that the names it threw up this time were their own. Neighbours had lost sons. Some of them were fellows Jim had been at school with. And his father felt, Jim thought, that his son ought to be lost as well. His father was bitter. Jim was depriving him of his chance to reach out and touch a unique thing, to feel that he too had dug into the new century and would not be repulsed.

'I'd go meself,' he insisted, 'if I wasn't so long in the tooth. To be with them *lads*! I'd give me right arm t' go!' And he punched hard at his open fist.

Only he wouldn't, Jim thought. He wouldn't be able to lift his left arm quick enough to keep up with his thirst.

Jim felt the ground tilting, as he had felt it that first day in Brisbane, to the place where the war was, and felt the drag upon him of all those deaths. The time would come when he wouldn't be able any longer to resist. He would slide with the rest. Down into the pit.

Later he was to think of that view from Bert's plane as his last vision of the world he knew, and of their momentarily losing sight of it when they turned to come down as the moment when he knew, quite certainly, that he would go. He didn't discuss it with anyone. But two weeks later, after having a few drinks in the pub and playing a slow game of pool, he rode up to Brisbane on the back of a fellow's motorbike – he didn't know the man, they had met only an hour before – and they both joined up.

If he didn't go, he had decided, he would never understand, when it was over, why his life and every-thing he had known were so changed, and nobody would be able to tell him. He would spend his whole life wondering what had happened to him and looking into the eyes of others to find out.

He strolled up to the house next morning and told Ashley Crowther. He didn't bother to tell his father.

Ashley nodded. They were sitting on their heels at the edge of the verandah, Jim chewing a match and Ashley, his eyes narrowed, gazing out over the paddocks, which glittered in the early morning chill. Now that the lower paddock had been ploughed and replanted, the Monuments could be seen, standing like ruined columns among the new shoots.

They didn't speak about Jim's work. It was left unstated that the job would be there for him when he got back. The birds could wait. The timespan for them was more or less infinite.

Miss Harcourt was not so easy. She seemed angry, but cheered up a little after they'd had tea.

'I'll hold the fort,' she said, making it sound the more heroic option.

He went the next day, and it was Miss Harcourt who rode up to the siding with him and waited to see him aboard. He stood looking at her out of the grimy window, her square grey figure among the coarse grass, with the smuts flying back in a cloud towards her as she swiftly receded. She was holding her bonnet on against the wind and clutching at it whenever she tried to raise her hand to wave.

Jim closed the window, already almost a soldier, and watched the beaten land go flat.

His father had got sentimental at the last. He had given Jim five quid and tried, as if he were still a child, to put his hand on the back of his neck, which was newly raw from the barber. It had made Jim, for a moment, see things differently, as if a line had been drawn between the past and what was to come, the two parts of his life, and he could look at all that other side clearly now that he was about to leave it. He still felt the weight of the old man's hand, its dry warmth, there on his neck and saw that his father would be alone now, maybe for good, and knew it. 'Agh!' he had said fiercely, 'you're the lucky one. To be goin'!'

Three months later, when his son was safely born, Ashley Crowther went as well, but as an officer, and in another division.

9

The world Jim found himself in was unlike anything he had ever known or imagined. It was as if he had taken a wrong turning in his sleep, arrived at the dark side of his head, and got stuck there.

Others were involved. Many thousands. And they were ordinary enough fellows like himself. They came from places back home with comfortable names like Samford and Bundaberg and Lismore over the border, and had obviously known similar lives since they spoke the same way he did and liked the same jokes and tunes. They were called Nobby Clarke, Blue Cotton, Jock McLaren, Cec Cope, Clem Battersby, and one of them was a stocky, curly-headed fellow called Clancy Parkett, who was always in trouble. He had first got into trouble on the induction course at Enoggera, then on the boat coming over, and had been in trouble ever since – he had slipped out with another bloke, on one of their first nights in France, and come back with two strangled chooks still flapping under his tunic. He knew some of the best stories Jim had ever heard, ran a poker school, and could down ten pints at a single session. Clancy teased Jim because Jim wanted, in his cautious way, to put every step down firmly and in the right place. Clancy was just the opposite. In real life, in Australia, he was an electrician.

Coming over on the *Borda*, and at Larkhill on Salisbury Plain while they were being trained and held back, there had been time enough to get to know one another and for every sort of hostility and friendship to develop. Jim made no close friends in the platoon, nobody special that is; but he thought of Clancy as someone he wouldn't want to be without. He might have been there always.

A lot of the men had wives and children and Jim had, over the months, seen their photographs and learned their names. Clancy had a List: addresses as well as names, which he flashed but never let you read. He also had stories about each of the women on his List – for a while he had done project jobs all over the southern part of the state – and Jim heard a good deal about a fisherman's wife up at the Passage, called Muriel, and others, a Pearl, a Maureen, at places like Warwick and Esk. It was the names of the places, as much as Clancy's ribald accounts of peace time philandering, that Jim liked to hear. It did him good, it kept the old life real; and he had no stories of his own to relate.

It was the same later when he and Bobby Cleese, after a trench raid, had spent a whole day and night together in a shell-hole in front of the lines, so close to the enemy out there that they could hear the striking of matches in the trenches up ahead and one man endlessly snuffling with a headcold. It was early February and the weather was freezing.

Bobby had talked of the Bay, in a low voiceless whisper that itself created mystery and made the familiar seem strange, as if dangerous or forbidden. He talked about fishing off Peel Island where the lepers were.

'Whiting now. that's a nice fish. Sweet. You can eat pounds of it if it's softly boiled with a white sauce and a bit of onion an' parsley in it. Bony, but. I saw a bloke choke once. It was horrible. The best place for whiting is over towards Redcliffe or round the point in Deception Bay. You ever been to Redcliffe, Jim? It's got a pier'.

Bobby's voice, white-breathed in the cold, evoked the whole blaze of the bay, faintly steaming (it would be summer there) in the heat before dawn, and Jim could see it, almost feel the warmth in his own bones, smell the dirty bilgewater in the bottom of the dinghy and feel fishscales drying and sticking to his feet. It was there, the Bay. It was daylight there. Even as they talked now, far out in no-man's land under the dangerous moon, it was dazzling with sunlight, or maybe building up to a storm that would only break in the late afternoon. Men would be out exercising greyhounds, and a milkcart with three metal cans might be starting on its rounds. Whiting, thousands of them, were swarming under the blue surface of Bob Cleese's eyes.

Jim would have liked then to speak of the swamp

and the big seas that would be running at this time of year, king tides they were called, all along the beaches, threatening to wash them away.

'Golly but I'm cold!' is what he muttered instead. The mud round the edge of the hole they were in was frozen solid. It had a razor-edge of dirty grey where the moon touched it. Ice. They were in mud to their knees and crouching.

'Tell us again, Bobby. About that bloke 'n the fish-bone. Deception.'

But more reassuring than all this – the places, the stories of a life that was continuous elsewhere – a kind of private reassurance for himself alone, was the presence of the birds, that allowed Jim to make a map in his head of how the parts of his life were connected, there and here, and to find his way back at times to a natural cycle of things that the birds still followed undisturbed.

Out on Salisbury Plain in the late summer and autumn there had been thousands of birds. And earlier in the year, when they first crossed the Channel, at le Havre, after the long train-trip from Marseilles, he had seen from the side of the ship a whole flock of sandpipers with their odd down-turned wings flying low over the greasy water, and among them, clearly distinguishable because so much bigger, knots, that would have been down from the arctic, their bodies reddish in that season – the same grey-crowned knots he might have seen along the coastal sandflats at home, arriving in spring and departing at the commencement of autumn, just as they did here. It was

61

comforting to see the familiar creatures, who might come and go all that way across the globe in the natural course of their lives, and to see that they were barely touched by the activity around them: the ferries pouring out smoke, the big ironclads unloading, the cries, the blowing of whistles, the men marching down the gangplanks and forming up on the quay, the revving of lorries, panicky horses being winched down, rearing and neighing, the skirl of Highland bagpipes. He noted the cry of these local sandpipers: *kitty wiper, kitty wiper*, which was new, and below them the cry of the knot, so familiar that he felt his heart turn over and might have been back in the warm dunes, barefoot, and in sight of a long fold of surf. *Thu thu* it went, a soft whistling. Then, more quietly, *wut*. Very low, though his ears caught it.

Still eager in those first days, he jotted all this down to be described later to Miss Harcourt. 'I have seen the dunlin' he was able to tell her. He had had no notion, from their single specimen, what they would look like in numbers. 'A great flock,' he wrote, 'twisting this way and that, all at once, very precise, with all the undersides flashing white on the turn.'

Back again at le Havre – it was winter now and they were camped on a greasy plain outside the port – Jim had been 'picked' by a big fellow from another company whose name was Wizzer Green.

He had never seen the man before. He didn't know what he had done, maybe he had done nothing at all, but something in him offended Wizzer, and while they were still wrought up after the crossing and tired after being marched up, there had been a bit of a fracas in which Wizzer tripped Jim and then accused him of deliberately getting in the way. In a moment they were eye to eye and preparing to fight.

There were no heated words. Wizzer's contemptuous challenge hadn't been heard by anyone else. But he and Jim had, at first sight almost, got to the bottom of one another. It could happen, it seemed⌈Jim had found himself defending whatever it was in him that Wizzer rejected, and discovered that he needed this sudden, unexpected confrontation to see who he was and what he had to defend. Enemies, like friends, told you who you were. They faced one another with murder in their eyes and Jim was surprised by the black anger he was possessed by and the dull savagery he sensed in the other man, whose square clenched brows and fiercely grinding jaw reminded Jim of his father – reminded him because he came closer to his father's nature at that moment than he had ever thought possible.⌉

It was Clancy who stepped between them, and before Jim knew quite what had happened it was Wizzer and Clancy who were slogging it out, but in a different spirit. Their violence was ordinary. They exchanged blows and insults and did and said all that was appropriate to such encounters, while other men gathered in a ring and cheered, but the occasion was not murderous as the earlier one had been. The others – all but Clancy – had backed away from that, recognizing a situation for which there were no rules.

The odd thing was that Wizzer seemed as relieved

as Jim to have the moment defused.

Clancy, who ended up merely clowning, got a black eye out of it and for days after he teased Jim and refused to let the matter drop.

'I'm wearing Jim Saddler's black eye,' he told people. But in no way suggested that Jim had ducked the issue; and nobody thought that. He had been ready enough to fight, ready even to kill.

Jim wondered about himself. When, afterwards, he left a wide circle round Wizzer Green, it wasn't out of timidity but from a wish not to be confronted with some depth in himself, and in the other man, that frightened him and which he did not understand.

10

They went up to Ballieul in cattle trucks, forty to a car. *Eight horses or forty men* the notice proclaimed. It seemed, even for the army, a rough equation and you wondered who had made it.

The loading took hours as the various companies were assembled beside their packs and then urged up into the wagons, the last men pushing in. It was cold at first, then hot, and the cars stank. Even after they had hung their packs up from hooks in the roof there wasn't enough room for them all to sit or sprawl. Many had to stand, pressed in hard against the walls.

These wagons had once taken cattle up to slaughter-houses. The old smell of the animals was still there in the wooden slats of the walls and in the scarred and trampled floor. They had gone up to the shambles in dumb terror. It was different with the men. After all those months in England, and the days in a holding camp at Ooostersteene, where they had been given gas-masks and taught to use them, they were impatient. Just to be moving was in itself something – that, and the knowledge that you were going to

65

arrive at last at the war. One fellow played a mouth-organ and they had a sing-song. But as the hours passed, twenty, twenty-four, and their limbs began to cramp, and they dried out with the sweating, and were slaked with thirst, it too became intolerable, this next stage, and they longed to get down, it didn't matter where.

Still, it wasn't all bad. You could slide the door open once you had found a place to settle, and if you didn't mind the cold, and see what sort of country you were moving into. There were roads off in the distance, some of them newly made, each with its own traffic, horses, guns with a carriage and limber, motor-lorries, occasionally a tractor, and columns of men marching in both directions, with officers on horseback ranging between.

The train slowed many times and jolted to a halt, its wheels grinding, and there was silence for a bit before the men began to curse. Some of them climbed down to piss beside the line; their piss steamed. One or two ran off into the snow and squatted, there seemed to be loads of time; and had to be hauled up again when the train, unpredictably, moved off. Clancy Parkett decided to get some hot water for tea, and while the wagons were still rolling slowly forward, he and Jim, leaving their rifles, jumped down and jogged along the whole length of the train till they came to the engine. They were racing it. Running easily in the soft French snow. Fellows leaned out of the wagons cheering. When they got there at last, Clancy, who was a bit on the heavy side, was too breathless to speak. It was

Jim, as they still jogged alongside, who told the driver what they wanted and showed the billy.

He was a big fellow with goggles and a moustache, in a blue boiler-suit. A Scot. He thought it very comic to see them jogging along and Clancy so breathless. He called the fireman out to look at them. The fireman, all stripped and sweatily begrimed, laughed out of his blackened face.

But they got the water, took it, all steaming as it was, on the run, then waited beside the track for their wagon and its familiar faces to re-appear. Jim held up the billy as if it were some sort of trophy, and as each wagon rolled by the men in it chiacked or cheered.

Jim would never have done any of it alone; but with Clancy it seemed like an adventure, a time out of all this that he would remember and maybe tell: the time I raced the train up to Ballieul with Clancy Parkett – his breathless conversation with the engine driver, the moment of simply standing all aglow in the cold, a spectator, while the faces of the whole battalion passed before them, and the land behind dipping away, foreign, mysterious, in snowy folds, crossed by black highways and tracks but empty of habitation. The tea when they gulped it down in sweet, steamy mouthfuls was especially good.

They were approaching the front. It was a new landscape now, newly developed for the promotion of the war. There were emergency roads everywhere, cutting across what must once have been vineyards or beet-fields, metalled for motor vehicles and guns, cobbled or packed with dirt for the men, and they were all in use, with men on foot or on horseback moving in dense columns, mules, horsed wagons, guns. Everywhere along the way there were blacksmith shops and dumps for ammunition, guarded enclosures containing spools of cable and great wheels of barbed wire, duckboards, sandbags, planking, solid beech-slabs for the new-style all-weather roads they were laying further up. Tramtracks ran between the roads, and telegraph-cables criss-crossed the earth or were being prepared for with deep slits. It was all in a state of intense activity. Things were being organized, you saw, on a large scale and with impressive expertise, as in the interests of an ambitious commercial project, the result of progress, efficiency and the increased potential of the age.

When they got down at last, on the outskirts of Ballieul, in the middle of the new landscape, Jim realized what it was he had been reminded of. It was a picture he had been shown, away back in Sunday school, of the building of the pyramids.

Large numbers of men, all roped together, were hauling blocks of stone up a slope, yoked together in thousands like cattle and hauling the blocks from every point of the compass towards a great cone that was rising slowly out of the sands. The fair-headed girl who was their teacher (she was called Agnes McNeill and later married a school-teacher) had drawn a moral from the picture: the Pharaohs were cruel (if you looked close you could see the overseers' whips) and ungodly, and their project was monstrous. But Jim, seeing the thing perhaps from the wrong perspective, and with the eyes of another century, had been impressed, as he was impressed now by the movement he saw all about him, vast numbers of men engaged in an endeavour that was clearly equal in scale to anything the Pharaohs had imagined and of which he, Jim Saddler, was about to become part.

11

It was a quiet section of the front. They were billeted in an abandoned cotton mill close to the centre of town. Though Armentiers by then had been fought over and taken and then retaken, and was frequently bombarded, it still retained a measure of normality; it hadn't as yet been gas-shelled and was not deserted. Girls appeared at the factory gate each morning with trays of buns and coffee; there were half a dozen good estaminets and several brothels; peasants on the outskirts of the town were still growing cabbages or trying to raise a wheatcrop right up to where the trenches began.

They were the local people whose farms had been where the war now was. They hadn't all left and they weren't all grateful that their land was being defended against invaders. Mostly they just wanted the war to move away. They were grim, wooden-faced people in clothes as muddy and ragged as the soldiers', their feet sometimes in clogs but more often in bundles of rags. They stood about on the doorsteps of shattered houses, defending their property – a few chickens, a cow, a cellar full of dusty bottles – against the defenders, who were always on the lookout for something to eat or steal, or for a woman who could be induced into one of the dirty barns, or for any sort of mischief that would kill boredom and take their minds off what lay ahead.

There were several wars going on here, and different areas of hostility, not all of them official.

As for the townspeople, they were like townspeople everywhere. The war was good business. The girls who sold cakes outside the cotton factory were pretty. Their mothers kept bars. Their younger brothers, in the afternoon, went up through the support lines to sell papers.

On the last night before they went into the line (they were to go up on December 23rd and spend Christmas there) Clancy prevailed on Jim to break bounds and go to a village just out of town. It was two miles off over the snow. It wasn't much of a place now, and probably never had been, but a woman kept a good estaminet there, in the shell of a bombed out farm-house, with eggs and sometimes cognac, and Clancy was on close terms with her. Though they had only been here a couple of weeks she was already on the List. Her name was Monique.

'Come on, mate, be a devil,' Clancy urged. 'We might all be dead by Christmas.'

Teasing Jim amused him. After all these months of raw camp life Jim still existed in a world of his own, not withdrawn exactly but impenetrably private. He did everything with meticulous care and according to the strict order of the book as if there were some peculiar safety in it, cleaning and swaddling his rifle, polishing his boots, laying out his kit. The odd thing was that Clancy respected this. It was what he saw in Jim that was most likeable and attractive. His drawing him out was a way of having Jim dig his heels in and be most earnestly himself.

'I tell yer, mate, in this world you've got t' work round the edge of things, the law, the rules. Creep up from behind. The straight way through never got a man nowhere.'

Jim dug in. 'No, Clancy. I reckon I'll stay.'

'Well Monique'll be disappointed. I promised 'er you'd be along. My mate Jim, I said. Next time up I'll bring my mate Jim.'

'The Captain –'

'Aw, bugger the Captain. D'y' think he cares? He makes the rules with 'is tongue in 'is cheek, the way he expects us t' keep 'em. Grow up mate! This is the real world. We're not the only ones, y' know. Half the battalion'll be there.'

Jim relented. It was, after all, their last night and the immediate future was unpredictable. They set out; but hadn't gone more than a hundred yards when there was a call behind them.

'Hey Jim, Clancy, where yous goin'?'

It was Eric Sawney, a pale, sad youth who from their very first day in Thompson's Paddock had latched on to Clancy and whose doglike devotion was a company joke. Clancy had found no way of discouraging the boy. Short of downright brutality Eric was not to be put off.

72

'Shit!' he said now, 'it's bloody Eric. I thought we'd lost 'im. They ought t' make that kid a police-dog.'

'Were yous goin'?' Eric repeated.

Clancy stood tugging his ear. 'Nowhere much, mate. We're just walkin' down our meal.'

'You're goin' into town,' the boy said, 'yous can't fool me. Can't I come?'

'Now Eric. Town is out of bounds at this hour. You know that. What'd y' mother say?'

'I havn' got a mother.'

'Well yer auntie then.'

Eric stuck. His drawn face, always pale, assumed a hard white look. He set his jaw somewhere between stubbornness and the sulks. Snow was falling.

'You're underage,' Clancy said desperately. 'I bet you're not sixteen.'

'I am so too. I'm eighteen.'

'Oh Jesus,' Clancy moaned. 'Come on then. But try not t' start a box on, eh mate? Keep that fierce temper a' yours under a bit of control.'

Clancy winked at Jim and Eric fell in beside them. Other groups, muffled against the cold, were up ahead, trudging on through the mud. There were more behind.

Monique was so unlike what Jim might have predicted that he wondered later about Muriel from the Passage and Phyllis, and Betty and Irene. She was a heavy blond woman of maybe fifty, sadly voluptuous, with bruised lips. She welcomed them all, let Clancy pinch her, and spent the rest of the evening resting her comfortable bosom on the counter or pouring slow drinks. Before long there were twenty or thirty of them, and later as many again from the 43rd. Two younger women, just girls really, came in to help fetch and carry and an old grannie with no teeth handled a big black pan, cooking omelettes and *pommes frites*. Clancy drank spirits, Jim and Eric *vin blanc* with syrup.

'Jesus,' Clancy protested, 'what is this? A kiddies' birthday do?'

But Jim craved the sweetness. For some reason, up here, he couldn't get enough of it. He blushed now to be in the same boat as Eric, who was always childishly whining for cakes and buns and whose pockets were full of squares of half-melted chocolate in silver paper for which he traded even his tobacco ration.

It was warm after a while, what with the crowd and the grog and the smoke from the pan. A Frenchman played a squeezebox. Jim got mildly drunk and Clancy got very drunk. Eric, wrapped up in his greatcoat and with his babyish mouth ajar, fell peacefully asleep.

'There mate, doesn't that feel good now? – a nice crowd, a woman leanin' on the bar.' Clancy had a talent for creating minor festivals out of almost nothing at all. Jim felt a great affection for him. 'I mean it's somethin' to remember isn' it, when we're up there freezin' our balls off all through Christmas. I remember last Christmas, I –' and Clancy was off on one of his stories. As usual Jim was soon lost in it. The wonders of Clancy Parkett's life. Only suddenly it turned in a direction he hadn't expected.

'Knocked me back,' Clancy was saying of some girl Jim had never been told about before and who didn't figure in the List. She had slipped into this particular story by stealth. Jim wondered if he hadn't, under the effects of the wine and the heat and Clancy's familiar voice, dozed off for a minute and missed her entry, till he saw that she had been in Clancy's sights all along, over there at the edge of what he was telling. He had, in his roundabout way, been leading up to her, but at the same time ignoring her presence, while he occupied himself with other things: the car he had driven last year, the places he went. He gave up at last and confronted her. 'Margaret,' he said, as if calling her in. 'Margaret she was called,' and immediately reddened all the way to the roots of his hair. Jim was astonished. The story had become a confession. 'So there you are. I joined up the next day.'

Jim didn't know what to say. He wasn't used to this sort of thing. He took another long swig of the sickly drink, then pushed it away from him; he'd had enough. Clancy gave Eric a shove and the boy started awake, grinning, then slept again.

'C'mon tiger,' Clancy said, hauling him upwards. Eric's eyes were closed and he was smiling blissfully. 'At least,' Clancy said, regarding the boy, 'if he's goin' t' get killed f' Christmas he'll 'v been pissed once in his life. Y' reckon you can walk, mate?'

'I can walk,' the boy said with sudden belligerence.

'All right, keep y' shirt on! I only asked.'

Next evening, after a day of anxious preparation, of cleaning and checking their kit and simply hanging about waiting, they made their way into the lines.

12

Often, as Jim later discovered, you entered the war through an ordinary looking gap in a hedge⌐ One minute you were in a ploughed field, with snowy troughs between ridges that marked old furrows and peasants off at the edge of it digging turnips or winter greens, and the next you were through the hedge and on duckboards, and although you could look back and still see farmers at work, or sullenly watching as the soldiers passed over their land and went slowly below ground, there was all the difference in the world between your state and theirs. They were in a field and very nearly at home. You were in the trench system that led to the war.⌐

But at Armentiers, on that first occasion, you came to the war from the centre of town. Crossing Half-past Eleven Square (it was called that because the Town Hall clock had stopped at that hour during an early bombardment; everything here had been renamed and then named again, as places and streets, a copse, a farmhouse, yielded up their old history and entered the new) you turned left and went on across Barbed-wire Square till you came to a big red building called the Gum-boot Store. There, after being fitted out with rubber boots that went all the way to mid-thigh, and tramping about for a few minutes to get used to the things, you were led away into the grounds of another, larger building, this time of brick, that was an Asylum; and from there, via Lunatic Lane, into the lines. Lunatic Lane began as a cobbled street, then became dirt, and before you quite knew it you were on planks. From this point the duckboards, for all their twisting and turning, led straight to the war.

They began to move up just at dusk, and by the time night fell and the first flares became visible, throwing their yellow glare on the underside of clouds and falling at times in a shower of brilliant stars, they were in the support line, stumbling in the dark through a maze of communication trenches, round firebays and traverses, jostling water-bottles, messtins, entrenching tools, grunting with the effort of trying to keep up, and quite blind except for the warning passed back from man to man of a hole up ahead in the greasy duckboards – *But where? How far? Am I almost on it?* – or a wire obstacle overhead.

The deeper they went the worse it got. In places where seepage was bad the duckboards were a foot under water. Once a whole earthwall had fallen and the passage was so narrow they could barely squeeze through: the place had been hit by a 'minnie'. They met two stretcher bearers moving in the opposite direction with a man who screamed, and some of the moisture, Jim thought, as they brushed in passing, must be blood. They hurried to keep up with the man in front and were soon breathless and sweating, partly because of the cracking pace that was being set – the men up front must actually have been running – but also because they were so keyed-up and eager to get there at last and see what it was. Everything here was so new, and they didn't know what might happen next, and when it did happen, how they would meet it. There was no stopping. If a man paused to adjust his pack or got his rifle caught in an overhead entanglement the whole troop might take a wrong turning and be lost in the dark.

The smell too got worse as they pushed further towards it. It was the smell of damp earthwalls and rotting planks, of mud impregnated with gas, of decaying corpses that had fallen in earlier battles and been incorporated now into the system itself, occasionally pushing out a hand or a booted foot, all ragged and black, not quite ingested; of rat-droppings, and piss, and the unwashed bodies of the men they were relieving, who also smelled like corpses, and were, in their heavy-eyed weariness as they came out, quite unrecognizable, though many of them were known to Jim by sight and some of them even by name; the war seemed immediately to have transformed them. They had occupied these trenches for eleven days. 'It's not so bad,' some of them mumbled, and others, with more bravado, claimed it was a cakewalk. But they looked beaten just the same.

They stayed eleven days themselves, and though the smell did not lessen, they ceased to notice it; it was their own. They were no longer the 'Eggs a-cook' of the easy taunt: 'Verra nice, verra sweet, verra clean. Two for one.' They were soldiers like the rest. They were men.

For eleven days they dug in and maintained the position. That is, they bailed out foul water, relaid duckboards, filled and carried sandbags to repair the parapet, stood to for a few minutes just before dawn with their rifles at the ready, crouched on the firestep, waiting – the day's one recognition of the reality of battle – then stood down again and had breakfast. Some days it rained and they simply sat in the rain and slept afterwards in mud. Other days it was fine. Men dozed on the firestep, read, played pontoon, or hunted for lice in their shirts. They were always cold and they never got enough sleep. They saw planes passing over in twos and threes, and occasionally caught the edge of a dogfight. Big black cannisters appeared in the sky overhead, rolling over and over, very slowly, then taking a downward path; the earth shook. You got used to that, and to the din.

Jim never saw a German, though they were there alright. Snipers. One fellow, too cocky, had looked over the parapet twice, being dared, and had his head shot off. His name was Stan Mackay, and it worried Jim that he couldn't fit a face to the name even when Clancy described the man. He felt he ought to be able to do that at least. A fellow he had talked to more than once oughtn't to just go out like that without a face.

Snipers. Also machine-gunners.

One of them, who must have had a sense of

humour, could produce all sorts of jazz rhythms and odd syncopations as he 'played' the parapet. They got to know his touch. Parapet Joe he was called. He had managed, that fellow, to break through and establish himself as something more than the enemy. He had become an individual, who had then of course to have a name. Did he know he was called Parapet Joe? Jim wondered about this, and wondered, because of the name, what the fellow looked like. But it would have been fatal to try and find out.

One night, for several hours, there was a bombardment that had them all huddled together with their arms around their heads, not just trying to stop the noise but pretending, as children might, to be invisible.

But the real enemy, the one that challenged them day and night and kept them permanently weary, was the stinking water that seeped endlessly out of the walls and rose up round their boots as if the whole trench system in this part of the country were slowly going under. Occasionally it created cave-ins, bringing old horrors back into the light. The dead seemed close then; they had to stop their noses. Once, in heavy rain, a hand reached out and touched Jim on the back of the neck. 'Cut it out, Clancy,' he had protested, hunching closer to the wall; and was touched again. It was the earth behind him, quietly moving. Suddenly it collapsed, and a whole corpse lurched out of the wall and hurled itself upon him. He had to disguise his tendency to shake then, though the other fellows made a joke of it; and two or three times afterwards, when he dozed off, even in sunlight, he felt the same hand brush his neck with its long curling nail, and his scalp bristled. Once again the dead man turned in his sleep.

Water was the real enemy, endlessly sweating from the walls and gleaming between the duckboard-slats, or falling steadily as rain. It rotted and dislodged A-frames, it made the trench a muddy trough. They fought the water that made their feet rot, and the earth that refused to keep its shape or stay still, each day destroying what they had just repaired; they fought sleeplessness and the dull despair that came from that, and from their being, for the first time, grimily unwashed, and having body lice that bred in the seams of their clothes, and bit and itched and infected when you scratched; and rats in the same field-grey as the invisible enemy, that were as big as cats and utterly fearless, skittering over your face in the dark, leaping out of knapsacks, darting in to take the very crusts from under your nose. The rats were fat because they fed on corpses, burrowing right into a man's guts or tumbling about in dozens in the bellies of horses. They fed. Then they skittered over your face in the dark. The guns, Jim felt, he would get used to; and the snipers' bullets that buried themselves regularly in the mud of the parapet walls. They meant you were opposed to other men, much like yourself, and suffering the same hardships. But the rats were another species. And for him they were familiars of death, creatures of the underworld, as birds were of life and the air. To come to terms with the rats, and his deep disgust for them, he would have had to turn his whole world upside down.

All that first time up the line was like some crazy camping trip under nightmare conditions, not like a war. There was no fight. They weren't called upon in any way to have a go.

But even an invisible enemy could kill.

It happened out of the lines, when they went back into support. Their section of D company had spent a long afternoon unloading ammunition-boxes and carrying them up. They had removed their tunics, despite the cold, and scattered about in groups in the thin sunlight, relaxed in their shirtsleeves, were preparing for tea. Jim sat astride a blasted trunk and was buttering slabs of bread, dreamily spreading them thick with golden-green melon and lemon jam. His favourite. He was waiting for Clancy to come up with water, and had just glanced up and seen Clancy, with the billy in one hand and a couple of mugs hooked from the other, dancing along in his bow-legged way about ten yards off. Jim dipped his knife in the tin and dreamily spread jam, enjoying the way it went over the butter, almost transparent, and the promise of thick, golden-green sweetness.

Suddenly the breath was knocked out of him. He was lifted bodily into the air, as if the stump he was astride had bucked like an angry steer, and flung hard upon the earth. Wet clods and buttered bread rained all about him. He had seen and heard nothing. When he managed at last to sit up, drawing new breath into his lungs, his skin burned and the effect in his eardrums was intolerable. He might have been halfway down a giant pipe that some fellow, some maniac, was belting over and over with a sledge hammer. *Thung. Thung. Thung.*

The ringing died away in time and he heard, from far off, but from very far off, a sound of screaming, and was surprised to see Eric Sawney, who had been nowhere in sight the moment before, not three yards away. His mouth was open and both his legs were off, one just above the knee, the other not far above the boot, which was lying on its own a little to the left. A pale fellow at any time, Eric was now the colour of butcher's paper, and the screams Jim could hear were coming from the hole of his mouth.

He became aware then of blood. He was lying in a pool of it. It must, he thought, be Eric's. It was very red, and when he put his hands down to raise himself from his half-sitting position, very sticky and warm.

Screams continued to come out of Eric, and when Jim got to his feet at last, unsteady but whole (his first thought was to stop Eric making that noise; only a second later did it occur to him that he should go to the boy's aid) he found that he was entirely covered with blood – his uniform, his face, his hair – he was drenched in it, it couldn't all be Eric's; and if it was his own he must be dead, and this standing up whole an illusion or the beginning of another life. The body's wholeness, he saw, was an image a man carried in his head. It might persist after the fact. He couldn't, in his stunned condition, puzzle this out. If it was the next life why could he hear Eric screaming out of the last one? And where was Clancy?

The truth hit him then with a force that was greater even than the breath from the 'minnie'. He tried to cry out but no sound came. It was hammered right back into his lungs and he thought he might choke on it.

[Clancy had been blasted out of existence. It was Clancy's blood that covered him, and the strange slime that was all over him had nothing to do with being born into another life but was what had been scattered when Clancy was turned inside out.]

He fell to his knees in the dirt and his screams came up without sound as a rush of vomit, and through it all he kept trying to cry out, till at last, after a few bubbly failures, his voice returned. He was still screaming when the others ran up.

He was ashamed then to have it revealed that he was quite unharmed, while Eric, who was merely dead white now and whimpering, had lost both his legs.

That was how the war first touched him. It was a month after they came over, a Saturday in February. He could never speak of it. And the hosing off never, in his own mind, left him clean. He woke from nightmares drenched in a wetness that dried and stuck and was more than his own sweat.

A few days later he went to sit with Eric at the hospital. He had never thought of Eric as anything but a nuisance, and remembered, a little regretfully now, how he and Clancy had tried to shake him off and how persistent he had been. But Clancy, behind a show of tolerant exasperation, had been fond of the boy, and Jim decided he ought, for Clancy's sake, to pay him a visit. He took a bar of chocolate. Eric accepted it meekly but without enthusiasm and hid it away under his pillow.

They talked about Clancy – there was nothing else – and he tried not to look at the place under the blanket where Eric's feet should have been, or at his pinched face. Eric looked scared, as if he were afraid of what might be done to him. *Isn't it done already?* Jim asked himself. *What more?*

'One thing I'm sorry about,' Eric said plaintively. 'I never learned to ride a bike.' He lay still with the pale sweat gathering on his upper lip. Then said abruptly: 'Listen, Jim, who's gunna look after me?'

'What?'

'When I get outa here. At home 'n all. I got no one. Just the fellers in the company, and none of 'em 'ave come to see me except you. I got nobody, not even an auntie. I'm an orfing. Who's gunna look after me, *back there?*'

The question was monstrous. Its largeness in the cramped space behind the screen, the way it lowered and made Eric sweat, the smallness of the boy's voice, as if even daring to ask might call down the wrath of unseen powers, put Jim into a panic. He didn't know the answer any more than Eric did and the question scared him. Faced with his losses, Eric had hit upon something fundamental. It was a question about the structure of the world they lived in and where they belonged in it, about who had power over them and what responsibility those agencies could be expected to assume. For all his childish petulance Eric had never been as helpless as he looked. His whining had been a weapon, and he had known how to make use of it. It was true that nobody paid any attention to him unless he wheedled and insisted and made a nuisance of himself, but the orphan had learned how to get what he needed: if not affection then at least a measure of tolerant regard. What scared him now was that people might simply walk off and forget him altogether. His view of things had been limited to those who stood in immediate relation to him, the matron at the orphanage, the sergeant and sergeant major, the sisters who ran the ward according to their own or the army's rules. Now he wanted to know what lay beyond.

'Who?' he insisted. The tip of his tongue appeared and passed very quickly over the dry lips.

Jim made a gesture. It was vague. 'Oh, they'll look after you alright Eric. They're bound to.'

But Eric was not convinced and Jim knew that his own hot panic had invaded the room. He wished Clancy was here. It was the sort of question Clancy might have been able to tackle; he had knocked about in the world and would have been bold enough to ask, and Jim saw that it was this capacity in Clancy that had constituted for Eric, as it had for him, the man's chief attraction: he knew his rights, he knew the ropes.

'I can't even stand up to take a piss,' Eric was telling him. The problem in Eric's mind was the number of years that might lie before him – sixty even. All those mornings when he would have to be helped into a chair.

'No,' Jim asserted, speaking now for the charity of

their people, 'they'll look after you alright.' He stood, preparing to leave.

'Y' reckon?'

'Of course they will.'

Eric shook his head. 'I don't know.'

'Wilya come again, Jim?' A fine line of sweat drops on the boy's upper lip gave him a phantom moustache. 'Wilya, Jim?' His voice sounded thin and far away.

Jim promised he would and meant it, but knew guiltily that he would not. It was Eric's questions he would be unable to face.

As he walked away the voice continued to call after him, aggrieved, insistent, 'Wilya, Jim'?. It was at first the voice of a child, and then, with hardly a change of tone, it was the voice of a querulous old man, who had asked for little and been given less and spent his whole life demanding his due.

Outside, for the first time since he was a kid, Jim cried, pushing his fists hard into his eye-sockets and trying to control his breath, and being startled – it was as if he had been taken over by some impersonal force that was weeping through him – by the harshness of his own sobs.

13

The air, even at knee height, was deadly. To be safe you had to stay at ground level on your belly, but safest of all was to be below ground altogether.

Breathless, and still trembling, his head numb with the noise that was rolling all about, Jim scrambled to the lip of the crater, and seeing even in the dark that there was no glint of water, went over the edge and slid. He struck something, another body, and recoiled. But in the sudden flash above the crater's rim saw that it was, after all, only a dead man. He had stopped being scared of the dead.

Making their way out here, crawling, moving on their knees, squirming at corpse level, they had seen dozens of unburied men, swollen black, their bellies burst, some with their pockets turned out white in the moonlight where the scavengers had been through. Jim had been happy to stay down among them while the air thumped and shuddered and occasional flashes revealed the thickets of barbed wire they had fallen among. The air was tormented. Dull axes might have been swinging down. An invisible forest, tree after tree, came crashing all about, you could feel the rush of breath as another giant hung a moment, severed from its roots, then slowly, but with gathering speed, came hurtling to the earth. Jim crawled among the dead. Occasionally one of them stirred and slithered forward; it was the only indication he had of there being others out here, still alive and moving on. There had been seventy of them at the start. But one of the officers who had brought them out was killed almost immediately and the other had got them lost. They were scattered all round among the wire and were no longer a group.

It was this sense of being alone out here that had broken him. That and a renewed burst of machine-gun fire that whipped up all the earth around and made an old corpse suddenly bounce and twitch. He had decided then that he'd had enough. He lay breathless for a moment, then slid into the shell-hole from which, he decided, he would not come out. He put his arms round his head, while the sky bumped and flickered and the deeper sound of shellfire was threaded through at moments with the chatter of the Maxims. He was out of it.

He lay back, breathing deep.

But now that he was safe again the wave of panic that had caught him up retreated a little and he saw that he would go back. He told himself that what he had stood quite well till just a moment ago he could stand again. Besides, it was dangerous to stay here and be left. He rolled on to his belly in a moving forward posture, gripped his rifle, and was about to spread his knees and push up over the rim, on to the live and dinning field, when his heel was caught from behind in an iron grip. He gave a yell, kicked out and tried to turn, and another hand grabbed his tunic. He was hauled back. He and his attacker rolled together towards the oozy bottom of the hole. Hoarsely protesting, punching out wildly in the dark, he began to fight.

It was eerie, nightmarish, to be fighting for your life like this in a shellhole out of the battle, and with an unknown assailant. They were locked fiercely, brutishly together, grunting strange words, trying to stagger upright enough to get the advantage, to get some force into their blows. The fight went on in the dark till they were groggily exhausted. Suddenly, in a flash of light, Jim saw who it was.

'Wizzer!' he found himself shouting as the man's hand continued to clutch at his throat, 'it's me, you mad bugger. Jim. A friend!' Wizzer seemed astonished. Falling back he threw Jim against the wall of the shell hole and Jim lay there, panting, with his heels dug in, and watched Wizzer draw a sweaty hand over his face, removing the mud. It was Wizzer alright, no doubt of it. Overhead the sky was split. A livid crack appeared in the continuity of things, a line of jagged light through which a new landscape might have been visible. The crack repeated itself as sound. Jim's head was split this time and the further landscape in there was impenetrably dark.

'What're you doing here?' Jim asked between breaths when they had recovered from this external assault.

Wizzer looked sly.

'What're you?'

Jim didn't know how to answer that.

'I sort of slipped,' he said.

Wizzer's face broke into a mocking grin, and Jim remembered with shame that only a few moments ago he had been cringing at the bottom of the hole with his head in his arms like a frightened child.

'You pulled me back,' he accused, suddenly misunderstood and self-righteous.

'Yair?'

'Listen Wizzer,' Jim began again, 'we've got t' get outa here and find the rest of the platoon.'

'Not me,' Wizzer said, springing to the alert. Just that, but Jim saw that he meant it, was in no way abashed, and assumed in his own frank admission of cowardice that they were two of a kind. Jim began to be alarmed. He tried in the dark to locate his rifle. He had stopped hearing the noise overhead. There were so many ways of being afraid; you couldn't be all of them at the same time.

'Listen Wizzer,' he said softly, as if reasoning with a child, 'this is serious. We're right out in the open here. Whatever happens we'll be for it. We're right out on our own.'

His fingers reached the rifle and he looked to the place where the sky began, wondering, if he took off, whether he could make it before Wizzer was on him again. He wanted nothing so much now as to be back where he had been ten minutes ago, in the thick of it. Scared silly, but not yet sullied.

Suddenly, alarmingly, Wizzer began to quake. His shoulders first, then his jaw. An odd moaning sound came from between the man's clenched teeth and Jim could see the whites of his eyes in the mud-streaked face. He had drawn himself up into a ball and was rocking back and forth, clenching his fists to his chest. His whole body was being shaken as by other, invisible hands.

Jim could have scrambled away without difficulty then, but was held. He felt a terrible temptation to join Wizzer in making that noise, in adding it to the whine and crack and thump of shellfire beyond the rim of the pit; it would be so liberating. But some sense of shame – for Wizzer, but also for himself – held him back from that and made it impossible also for him to slip away.

'This is terrible,' he said to nobody, standing upright now, knee-keep in the mud they had churned up. He didn't know what to do. Wizzer had subsided into choking sobs. The other had let him go.

'Listen Wizzer,' he said, 'I'm leaving now. Alright, mate? If you want to come with me we could go together. But it's alright if you don't.' He backed away to the wall of the hole and dug in ready to climb. 'Alright Wizzer? Alright?'

He felt desperately unhappy. He really did want Wizzer to come; it was the only way to wipe all this clean. He kept his eye on the man, who was still again, with his head lifted like an animal and keenly observing, as if Jim were doing something incomprehensibly strange. Jim eased himself up towards the edge of the pit. 'I wish,' he said, 'I wish you'd come Wizzer.' But

92

the other man shook his head. With one last look backwards Jim rolled over and out, and was immediately back on the field, in that weird landscape as you saw it at belly level of wire entanglements, smashed trees, the knees of corpses, and other, living figures, some quite close, who were emerging like himself from shallow holes. He was back.

He began, half-crouching, to move ahead. It was like advancing into a bee-swarm. The air was alive with hot rushing bodies that knifed down and swung hissing round his ears.

'Is that you Jim?'

It was Bobby Cleese. He was never so glad to see anyone in his life.

He scrambled to Bobby's side and they started forward together, then with fiery stars chopping at the earth again, they fell, together with others, who had also appeared as if from nowhere, into a wet ditch. From there Jim could see more of their lot over to the right.

So he wasn't lost after all. He had found the company, and might have considered his time out of all this a dream, a fear of what he might do rather than what he had done, if it weren't for Wizzer. Wizzer's face, and Wizzer's grip on him when they had wrestled together in the mud, were too real, and too humbling in his memory, to be dismissed.

'I was scared silly back there,' he whispered into Bob Cleese's shoulder. He needed to go forward now with a clear conscience.

'You were scared,' Bob said, and they both giggled.

Jim felt himself delivered into his own hands again, clean and whole – what did it matter if he got killed? – and discovered a great warmth in his heart for this fellow Bob Cleese, whom he had barely known till now. He was a bee-keeper back home. That was all Jim knew of him. A thin, quiet fellow from Buderim, and it occurred to him as they lay there that they might understand one another pretty well if there was a time after this when they could talk. Everything here happened so quickly. Men presented themselves abruptly in the light of friends or enemies and before you knew what had happened they were gone. Wizzer! It was odd to recall that not much more than a year ago he had been waiting, in what he thought of as a hypnotized state, for life to declare itself to him and make its demands.

Meanwhile, one of the others in the ditch had turned out to be an officer. Jim didn't believe he had ever seen the boy before, but he must have; it was the light. He was one of those fellows who were always clean. Even out here in the mud he looked perfectly brushed and scrubbed. His round face shone.

'Listen men,' he whispered, lifting his chin. He seemed filled with boyish nobility, playing his part of the junior officer as he had learned from the stories in *Chums*. He was very convincing. 'We're going forward, right?'

'It's a mistake,' Jim thought, whose own youth lay so far back now that he could barely recall it. 'This kid can't be more than twelve years old.' But when the voice said 'Right men, now!' he rose up out of the ditch and followed.

The boy was immediately hit, punched in the belly by an invisible fist and propelled abruptly backward. He looked surprised. 'Unfair!' his blue eyes protested. 'I wasn't ready. Unfair!' He turned regretfully away, but Jim had no opportunity to see him fall. He had already thrown himself into yet another shallow hole and was, this time, with two quite different men. Bob Cleese was ahead somewhere, or maybe behind.

'Will it be like this,' he wondered, 'all the way to Berlin?'

It was later, after another brief rush forward, that he and Bobby Cleese found themselves in the same shell-hole and were stranded there all night and all the next day as well, not twenty feet from the German lines. So they did have time, after all, and that night, and all the next day, they could hear Germans shifting their feet on the duckboards, striking matches to light their pipes, rambling in their sleep, and behind them, in no man's land, their own wounded groaning or crying out for help. To shut out the sounds, and to keep their spirits up, Bob Cleese had told about the fishing at Deception in a low, calm voice that quieted in Jim a swarm of confused terrors and set them smokily asleep.

It might have seemed, as the day wore on, that they would never get out. But they forgot that as their limbs unfroze at last in the yellow sunlight. The smoke of cookfires trickled up. They smelled bacon. And men could be heard going about their peaceable daylight tasks. Birds appeared, and Jim shyly identified them. In the afternoon they slept. Once you put to one side

95

the notion of the danger you were in, and the possibility when night returned of sudden death, it was almost idyllic that long afternoon in the sun and the whispered talk.

They got back that time. It was later, much later, in June, that Bobby Cleese died. But by then more than a third of the battalion had disappeared and been replaced. Jim was a veteran. He had fought in every part of the line around Armentiers: at Houplines on the L'Epinette salient, at Ploegsteert, at le Bizet. He had been in a great battle.

It was while they were at Pont de Nieppe, waiting to come up to the battle, that Bobby Cleese was killed. The Germans shelled their billets with gas-shells, first tear gas, then phosgene. There was utter confusion and they had to abandon the town and sleep in the fields. Bob Cleese got a bad dose but didn't die till two days later.

Jim's company, by then, had been led in the dark through a maze of trenches to their old position at Bunkhill Row, and it was from there, just before dawn, that he saw the mines go up. The whole earth suddenly quaked under their feet as if an express train were rushing along below. There was a mighty roar. A cloud that bore no relation to the sound began slowly to rise westward. Like a pink and yellow rose made of luminous dust, it bloomed above the skyline, and climbed and climbed, till the sky in that quarter was entirely choked. It turned grey, and its smell as it withered was of charred flesh. When the smoke dispersed at last the landscape on every side was touched with flame. One whole hillside, over towards Hollebeke, beyond what remained of Ploegsteert wood, lay open and aglow, as if the door of a blast furnace had been thrown open and the horizon all round was lit with the reflection of it. It was like the mouth of hell. They rose up on a signal and poured into it.

Two days later, when they pulled out of the lines again, Jim got permission to go up to the hospital and find Bob.

It was a fine warm day, and in the aftermath of something very like a victory a holiday atmosphere prevailed. Weary men were making their way back out of the lines and many were wounded; others, more cruelly maimed, rode in closed wagons and you could hear their groans; but they were moving away from the battle zone into cleaner air and a glimpse of green and that made all the difference. The great pall of yellow smoke that hung over the battle-lines was well behind them and the sky ahead was blue. Jim especially felt light-footed and easy, and was happy to be striding out on his own with a twelve-hour pass in his pocket and the prospect of seeing his friend. He walked at first, in a great press of men, then accepted a lift on the back of a lorry, then further along rode for a bit on one of the guns. He met a blond fellow with no teeth who tried to sell him a safety razor. Another bearded soldier, very dirty and with no distinguishing tabs on his uniform, which seemed all odds and ends of other men's castoffs, had a stack of things on a groundsheet whose praises he sang in a high sing-song voice like a spruiker at the Show. There

.

was a Mills bomb, a Prussian helmet with a bullet-hole in it, two watches, one with a metal band, a blue neckerchief, a revolver, a torch and a very real-looking glass eye. Jim didn't want any of these things, nor the gold fillings the man showed him in his dirty palm, but he inspected them along with others and wondered that the man had time for so much private industry. He accepted another lift in a field ambulance and played a short game of blackjack with two stretcher-bearers, who lost a shilling apiece. It was when he got down from the ambulance, just on the outskirts of the hospital, that he saw the crowd, and approaching the edges of it and pushing through was presented with something marvellous.

The men who had been mining under Hill 60, just a few days earlier, had discovered the fossil of a prehistoric animal, a mammoth, together with the flints that had been used either to kill or to cut it up. Very carefully, in the rush to get the galleries finished before the Germans finished theirs (for the two lots of miners had for several weeks been tunnelling in one anothers' path) the fossil had been uncovered and brought out, and now, with the battle barely over and the dead still being counted (fifty thousand, they said, on the German side alone) it was waiting to be conveyed behind the lines and examined by experts.

It was a great wonder, and Jim stared along with the rest. A mammoth, thousands of years old. Thousands of years dead. It went back to the beginning, and was here, this giant beast that had fallen to his knees so long ago, among the recent dead, with the sharp little flints laid out beside it which were also a beginning. Looking at them made time seem meaningless. Jim raised his eyes to the faces – intent, puzzled, idly indifferent – of the other men who had been drawn here, but they seemed no better able to understand the thing than himself. Some of them had come directly from the lines. Turning aside a moment, they regarded the creature out of crusted eyes as if it were one of themselves: more bones. Others, who could look at things from the distance that came with a fresh uniform and the brief absence of vermin, might be seeing it as it was intended to be seen, a proof that even here among the horrors of battle a spirit of scientific enquiry could be pursued, its interests standing over and above the particular circumstances of war, speaking for a civilization that contained them all, British and German alike, and to which they would return when the fighting was done.

In a field tent up at the hospital, where the dying were kept apart from the rest, Bob Cleese was in the final stages, fevered beyond hope. Jim regarded him with horror and was ashamed that he should feel disgust. Under Bob's mild eyes, where the whiting had swarmed, gathered the yellow pints of fluid he was spewing up out of his lungs, four pints every hour for the past twenty-four. Jim stared and couldn't believe what he saw. Yellow, thick, foul-smelling, the stuff came pouring out, and poured and poured, while Bob's eyes bulged and he choked and groaned. At last a nurse came, and gently at first, then roughly, she pushed Jim away. The whole tent was filled with such cases. The noise and the smell were terrible. Only the dead were quiet, lying stiff and yellow on their frames. Outside at last, Jim staggered in the sunlight and gulped for breath. He began to walk back towards the front, under the great yellow pall that in all that quarter hung low over the earth.

That night they went back into the lines, and for five days and nights they dug in and defended themselves against counter attacks and were bombed and machine-gunned from planes and lived in the stench of the German dead. Two weeks later they were back. For eighteen days. They were half-crazy that time, and once, digging furiously, while the sky cracked and blazed and men all round were being sliced with shrapnel or, with an entrenching tool floating high above them, were lifted clean off their feet and suspended a moment in mid-air, Jim felt his shovel scrape against bone and slice clean through a skull. He heard teeth scrape against metal, and his own teeth ground in his head. But he dug just the same, and the corpse, which had been curled up knee to chin and fist to cheekbone was quickly uncovered and thrown aside.

He had begun to feel immeasurably old. Almost everyone he had known well in the company was gone now and had been twice replaced. The replacements came up in new uniforms, very nice, very sweet, very clean, and looked like play soldiers, utterly unreal, till they too took on the colour of the earth or sank below it. It was like living through whole generations. Even the names they had given to positions they had held a month before had been changed by the time they came back, as they had changed some names and inherited others from the men who went before. In rapid succession, generation after generation, they passed over the landscape. Marwood Copse one place was called, where not a stick remained of what might, months or centuries back, have been a densely-populated wood. When they entered the lines up at Ploegsteert and found the various trenches called Piccadilly, Hyde Park Corner, the Strand, it was to Jim, who had never seen London, as if this maze of muddy ditches was all that remained of a great city. Time, even in the dimension of his own life, had lost all meaning for him.]

14

Going up now was a nightmare. It was late summer and the roads, in the scorching heat, were rivers of dust filled with the sound of feet falling on planks, the rumble of gun-carriages and lorries, the jingling of chains, the neighing of horses, a terrible clamour; and when the rain fell, and continued to fall as it did for days on end, they were a sea of mud into which everything was in danger of sinking without trace and which stank of what it had already swallowed, corpses, the bloated carcasses of mules, horses, men.

Packed again into a cattletruck, pushed in hard against the wall, in the smell of what he now understood, Jim had a fearful vision. It would go on forever. The war, or something like it with a different name, would go on growing out from here till the whole earth was involved; the immense and murderous machine that was in operation up ahead would require more and more men to work it, more and more blood to keep it running; it was no longer in control. The cattletrucks would keep on right across the century, and when there were no more young men to fill them they would be filled with the old, and with women and children. They had fallen, he and his contemporaries, into a dark pocket of time from which there was no escape.

Jim saw that he had been living, till he came here, in a state of dangerous innocence. The world when you looked from both sides was quite other than a placid, slow-moving dream, without change of climate or colour and with time and place for all. He had been blind.

It wasn't that violence had no part in what he had known back there; but he had believed it to be extraordinary. When he was fifteen years old his younger brother, who was riding on the guard of a harvester he was driving, and singing over the tops of the wheat in his babyish voice *I'm the king of the castle, you're the dirty rascal*, had suddenly lost his footing and tipped backwards into the blades. Jim had run a half mile through the swath he had cut in the standing grain with the image in his head of the child caught there among the smashed stalks and bloodied ears of wheat, and been unable when he arrived at the McLaren's door to get the image, it so filled him, into words. There were no words for it, then or ever, and the ones that came said nothing of the sound the metal had made striking the child's skull, or the shocking whiteness he had seen of stripped bone, and would never be fitted in any language to the inhuman shriek – he had thought it was some new and unknown bird entering the field – of the boy's first cry. It had gone down, that sound, to become part of what was unspoken between them at every meal so long as his mother was still living and

103

they retained some notion of being a family. He had never been able to talk to her of it and she had died looking past him to the face of the younger boy; and still they hadn't talked.

There was that. And there was a kestrel he had found once with a tin tied to its leg, a rolled-up sardine-tin still with its key. He had wept with rage and pain at the cruelty of the thing, the mean and senseless cruelty. His hands had been torn by the bird, which couldn't distinguish between kindness and more cruelty, and afterwards when it flapped away he had sat with his bloodied hands between his knees and thought of his brother. *There*, something in him had said. *There*! But he had freed only one small life, and the kestrel, with the weight of the sardine-tin gone but still there, and the obscene rusty object lying in the dirt where Jim had kicked it, was too sick from starvation to do more than flop about in the grass and would only feebly recover its balance in the air.

That was how it was, even in sunlight. Even there.

What can stand, he asked himself, what can ever stand against it? A ploughed hillside with all the clods gleaming where the share had cut? A keen eye for the difference, minute but actual, between two species of wren that spoke for a whole history of divergent lives? Worth recording in all this? He no longer thought so. Nothing counted. The disintegrating power of that cruelty in metallic form, when it hurled itself against you, raised you aloft, thumped you down like a sack of grain, scattered you as bloody rain, or opened you up to its own infinite blackness – nothing stood before

104

that. It was annihilating. It was all.

Last time he had come up here there had been peasants in the field. Now the area behind the lines was utterly blasted. The earth was one vast rag and bone shop, the scattered remains of both sides lay all over it: shell fragments and whole shells of every size, dangerously unexploded, old sandbags trodden into the mud, a clasp and length of webbing, the head of an entrenching tool, buckled snapshots, playing cards, cigarette packets, pages of cheap novels and leaflets printed in English, German, French, scraps of wrapping-paper, bent tableforks and spoons, odd tatters of cloth that might be field-grey or horizon-blue or khaki, you could no longer tell which; smashed water-bottles, dented cups, odd bits of humanity still adhering to metal or cloth or wood, or floating in the green scum of shell-holes or spewed up out of the mouths of rats. They made their way across it. Once again they dug in.

One day when his company was back in support he was sent out with a dozen others to look for firewood in what remained of a shattered forest. All the leaves had been blasted from the trees and they stood bare, their trunks snapped like matchwood, their branches jagged, split, or broken off raw and hanging. They were astonished, coming into a clearing at the centre of it, to see an old man in baggy pants and braces digging.

A grave it must be, Jim thought. When the man plunged his spade in for the last time and left it there it had the aspect of some weird, unhallowed cross.

But it wasn't a grave. The bit of earth he had dug was larger than a body would require.

The old man, who did not acknowledge their presence, had taken up a hoe and was preparing the earth in rows. It was the time for winter sowing, as any farmer among them would know, but it was a measure of the strangeness of all things here, of the inversion of all that was normal, that they saw immediately from what he was doing that the man was crazy. One of the fellows called out to him but he did not look up.

They moved round the edge of the wood gathering splinters for kindling, and Jim, as he stood watching the man for a moment with a great armful, thought of Miss Harcourt, whom he hadn't remembered for days now. There was something in the old man's movements as he stooped and pushed his thumbs into the earth, something in his refusal to accept the limiting nature of conditions, that vividly recalled her and for a moment lifted his spirits. So that later, by another reversal, whenever he thought of Miss Harcourt he was reminded of the man, stooped, pressing into the earth what might by now be a crop of French beans or turnips or beets; though in fact they never went back to the place – Jim didn't even know where it was, since they never saw a map – and he had no opportunity of observing what the old man had been planting or whether it had survived.

Shortly after that, however, to keep hold of himself and of the old life that he had come close to losing, he went back to his notes. Even here, in the thick of the fighting, there were birds. The need to record their

106

presence imposed itself on him as a kind of duty.

Saturday: a wryneck, with its funny flight, up and down in waves, the banded tail quite clear.

Wednesday: larks, singing high up and tumbling, not at all scared by the sound of gunfire. Skylarks. They are so tame that when they are on the ground you can get real close and see the upswept crest. I am training myself to hear the different sound of their flight paths; the skylarks that fly straight up and tumble and the woodlarks that make loops like Bert in his plane. The songs are similar but different because of the path.

Friday: a yellow wagtail. Can it be? Like the yellow wagtail we saw once at Burleigh that Miss Harcourt photographed. I wish I had the picture to compare. The sound I remember quite well. *Tseep, tseep*. The same yellow stripe over the eye. Or have I forgotten?

It was by then October. One night, lying awake in the old cemetery where they were bivouacked, just outside Ypres, he saw great flocks of birds making their way south against the moon. Greylag geese. He heard their cries, high, high up, as they moved fast in clear echelons on their old course. When he fell asleep they were still flying, and when he woke it was to the first autumn rains. All the damp ground, with its toppled stones, was sodden, and the men, lying among them or already up and preparing to move, were covered with the thick Flemish mud that stretched now as far as the eye could see and entirely filled the view.

15

The men, having stacked their rifles in neat piles and removed their packs, were taking their rest beside the road or had staggered off to where yellow flags marked the newly-dug latrines.

It was all so orderly and followed so carefully what was laid down in the book that it was difficult to believe, till you saw the racked and weary faces of the men, or observed the pain with which they lowered themselves to the earth, that they had already marched twelve miles this morning and were at the end of their endurance; or till you saw the terrible traffic that was moving in the opposite direction – sleep-walking battle survivors, walking wounded, men hideously mutilated and bloody, in lorries, wagons, handcarts – that there was a battle raging up ahead and that these men were making towards it with all possible speed; that is, at the precise rate, three miles an hour, with ten minutes rest for every fifty moving, that was laid down for the exercise in the army manual. Ashley Crowther knew these things because he was an officer and it was his business to know. He looked and marvelled. First at the men's power to endure, then at the army's deep and awful wisdom in these matters: the logistics of battle and the precise breaking point of men.

The traffic moved in a long cloud. Brakes crashed, horsechains clattered, men in the death wagons groaned or screamed as the rigid wheels bumped over ruts. Officers shouted orders. His own men simply lay scattered about in the dusty grass at the side of the road; prone, sprawled, dead beat. Very nearly dead.

A little way back they had passed the ruins of a village and he had been surprised to see that there were still peasants about. He saw a boy of nine or ten, very pale with red hands, who milked a cow, resting his cropped head against the animal's sunken ribs as he pulled and pulled. Ashley had looked back over his shoulder at the scene, but the boy, who was used to this traffic, as was the cow, had not looked up.

Later, on the outskirts of another group of blasted farms, he saw a man mending a hoe. He had cut a new handle and was carefully shaping it with a knife, bent over his simple task and utterly absorbed, as if the road before him were empty and the sky overhead were also empty, not dense with smoky thunder or enlivened at odd, dangerous moments with wings. Did the man believe the coming battle was the end and that he might soon have need of the hoe?

That had been at their last resting-place; and Ashley, while he lay and smoked, had watched the man shape and test the handle, peeling off thin slivers and rubbing his broad thumb along the grain. He was still at it, minutes later, when they moved on.

There were so many worlds. They were all continuous with one another and went on simultaneously: that man's world, intent on his ancient business with the hoe; his own world, committed to bringing these men up to a battle; their worlds, each one, about which he could only guess.

They were resting now, given over as deeply and as quickly as possible to sleep. In three more minutes they would be lumbering out to take their places on the road. By morning –.

A few miles away, behind concrete emplacements, the machine guns were already set up waiting. The deadly sewing-machines were stitching their shrouds.

He was profoundly weary of all this. Once or twice during his years at Cambridge he had spent a hunting weekend at Gem Oliver's place in Shropshire. They had sat in bunkers in the woods while beaters drove the small game towards them, and fired and fired, watching the creatures spring up and turn somersaults in the air or roll away twitching. It was like that out here. The men, scarcely believing they could be walking upright at last, and in daylight, in a place where they had always gone on their bellies by night, would move in ragged lines towards the guns, and in a flickered chattering dream, as the bullets whipped the air all about them or following their own trajectory, passed magically through, would, after seconds some, and minutes others, go down in waves under the whistling blades and lie randomly about, as they did now in the relative quiet of the grass.

Ashley blew his whistle. Slowly, as in a dream, the men rose and stumbled into the road.

He was surprised as always, as they came to attention, to find that they harboured within them, these peaceable farmers, cattlemen, clerks, plumbers, pastry-cooks, ice-men, shop-assistants, and those who had never done more than hang about billiard parlours or carry tips to race-courses, or sport flash clothes in city pushes, the soldier – hard, reliable, efficient – they could so smartly become. The transformation was remarkable.

It wasn't simply the uniform, though that was the mark of it; or the creation through drilling of a general man from whom all private and personal qualities had been removed. The civilian in these men survived. You saw it in the way a man wore his hat, or in the bit of cloth he chose – an old shirt-tail or singlet, a roll of flannel, a sock – to protect the bolt of his rifle. You heard it in the individual tilt of his voice through even the most conventional order or response. It was the guarantee that they would, one day, cease to be soldiers and go back to being school-teachers, mechanics, factory-hands, race-course touts.

It had happened to him as well. He had quite unexpectedly discovered in himself, lurking there under the floral waistcoat and his grandfather's watch-chain, the lineaments of an officer. He was calm, he kept his head; he kept an eye out for his men; they trusted him. He was also extraordinarily lucky, and being lucky had seen many men over these months, whose luck wasn't as good as his own, go down. This new lot –

111

who started out now as he gave the signal and the line began to move – they too would go down. They were 'troops' who were about to be 'thrown in', 'men' in some general's larger plan, 're-enforcements', and would soon be 'casualties'. They were also Spud, Snow, Skeeter, Blue, Tommo. Even he had a nick-name. It had emerged to surprise him with its corres-pondence to something deep within that he hadn't known was there till some wit, endowed with native cheek and a rare folk wisdom, had offered it to him as a gift. He was grateful. It was like a new identity. The war had remade him as it had remade these others. Not forever, but in a way he would never entirely outgrow.

Ashley, whose mind was of the generalizing sort, had seen quite clearly from the beginning that what was in process here was the emergence of a new set of conditions. Nothing after this would ever be the same. War was being developed as a branch of industry. Later, what had been learned on the battlefield would travel back, and industry from now on, maybe all life, would be organised like war. The coming battle would not be the end, even if it was decisive; it was another stage in the process.

It seemed more important than ever now to hang on to the names, the nicknames, including his own, and if his luck held, to go back. And having learned at last what the terms were – and in expiation of the blood that was on his hands – to resist.

16

Jim leaned, half-sitting, half-lying, against the wall
of the ditch, glad to feel the earth against his cheek,
and also his shoulder, as he waited rifle in hand for the
whistle that would take them in.

They had come up in the dark following a white
tape, and stakes, also white, that had been driven into
the ground but washed out overnight by a storm.
After weeks of hot dusty weather the rains had come
and the earth was sodden and astream. Just an hour
ago there had been a bombardment. So many men
were killed in the rear line that the companies being
held there had been brought up with the rest, and they
were all packed now into the same narrow space, a
terrible press of men, stunned, anxious, elated, solemnly waiting.

Jim looked down the line of men who half-stood,
half-sprawled against the opposite wall. It was like
seeing his own group repeated in a glass, or like looking at the wall itself, since the men, their uniforms all
caked in mud, seemed little more in the dim light than
another wall built up out of faces with deep ruts in

them and rocklike, stubbled jaws, skin greasily shin-
ing where it was drawn over the skullbones, knuckles
grained with dirt, coarse-grained necks above collars
grimed at the edge, the cloth of the uniforms also
coarse, and like the faces all of one colour, the earth-
colour that allows a man to disappear un-noticed into
the landscape, or to pass through, hunched shoulders, flexed knee and elbow, into a wall.

But the wall was in motion, even in its stillness. The
bodies were not all here. His own wasn't. Some of
them were in the past and in another country; others
might already have leapt the next few minutes into the
future, and were out in the firestorm, or had got
beyond even that to some calm green day on the other
side of it. Those who were stolidly here in the present
had gone deep inside themselves and were coming to
terms with the blood as it rolled round and round from
skull to foot, still miraculously flowing in its old
course; or with that coldness in the pit of the stomach
that no rum could touch; or that shrinking in the groin
as belts were tightened, that withdrawal of their own
most private parts, that said: *No further, the line ends
here*. They were communing with themselves in words
out of old nursery prayers, naming the names of those
they had been instructed to pray for, the loved-ones;
they were coaxing themselves, cheering themselves
up, using always their own names, but as they had
heard it when they were so young that it still seemed
new and un-repeatable; holding at bay on their breath
that other form of words, the anti-breath of a back-
ward-spelled charm, the no-name of extinction, that if

allowed to take real shape there might make its way deep into the muscles or find a lurking place in the darkest cells. *No, I am not going to die.*

One fellow, with calm grey eyes and a thin mouth, was smoking. Pale clouds drifted before him, greyer than his face, and his eyes were like flints in a wall. He cupped his hand and drew again on the cloud-machine. Another long drift, smoky-grey. And behind it the hand that was square and solid earth.

I am getting too far ahead, Jim thought. *That is for later. I should get back to where I am.*

None of this came to him as so many words. He perceived it or it unfolded in him. What he saw in clear fact was a line of children, sleepily and soberly intent, who waited with their knees drawn up for a journey to resume after a minor halt. He thought that because the place where they were waiting had been a station on the line from Menin to Ypres. Children might once have waited here on slow trips to the city. He closed his eyes and could have slept.

He felt out of himself.

It wasn't the rum; there wasn't enough of it for that – one mouthful, warm as blood. He had felt this way before with odd parts of his body. His feet, for example. In the intense cold of the winter they had sometimes seemed a thousand miles off, ten thousand even, and quite beyond reach. He had thought of them as having got sick of all this, as having made their way home without him, and had imagined them leaving their bare prints on sand, among gull-feathers, cuttle-shells and the three-toed scratch marks of oys-

115

tercatchers beside the surf.

This was different. It was the whole of him.⌐

He was perfectly awake and clear-headed, aware of the rough cloth of his uniform, the weight of his pack, the sweat and stink of himself that was partly fear; but at the same time, even as he heard the whistle and rose to scramble over the lip of the ditch, taking the full weight of pack, rifle, uniform, boots, and moved on into the medley of sound, he was out of himself and floating, seeing the scene from high up as it might look from Bert's bi-plane, remote and silent. Perhaps he had, in some part of himself, taken on the nature of a bird; though it was with a human eye that he saw, and his body, still entirely his own, was lumbering along below, clearly perceptible as it leapt over potholes and stumbled past clods, in a breathless dream of black hail striking all about him and bodies springing backward or falling slowly from his side. There were no changes. But he moved in one place and saw things from another, and saw too, from up there, in a grand sweep, the whole landscape through which he was moving: the irregular lines of trenches that made no sense at ground level, the one he had left and the one, all staggered pill-boxes, that they were making for, where the machine guns were set that spilled out lines of fire and chop-chopped at the air. The land between, over which they were running, was all flooded ruts and holes, smashed branches, piles of shattered cement. But from high up, with all its irregularities ironed out, it might appear as a stretch of quite ordinary country, green in spots and sodden with rain,

116

over which small creatures were incomprehensibly running and falling, a bunched and solid mass that began to break up and develop spaces like a thinning cloud.

He saw it all, and himself a distant, slow-moving figure within it: the long view of all their lives, including his own – all those who were running, half-crouched, towards the guns, and the men who were firing them; those who had fallen and were noisily dying; the new and the old dead; his own life neither more nor less important than the rest, even in his own vision of the thing, but unique because it was his head that contained it and in his view that all these balanced lives for a moment existed: the men going about their strange business of killing and being killed, but also the rats, the woodlice under logs, a snail that might be climbing up a stalk, quite deaf to the sounds of battle, an odd bird or two, like the couple of wheatears he had seen once in a field much like this, the male with his grey back and crown, the female brownish, who had spent a whole morning darting about on the open ground while he lay with a pair of borrowed field-glasses screwed into his head and lost himself in their little lives, in their ordinary domestic arrangements, as now, stumbling forward, he was, in a different way, lost in his own.

He continued to run. Astonished that he could hold all this in his head at the same time and how the map he carried there had so immensely expanded.

17

Suddenly, as it seemed, though several minutes must have passed, he found himself on the ground looking up at blue sky in which clouds moved so slowly that he blinked and then blinked again before he could be certain that they were not altogether stopped.

He drifted with them. He watched them tease out, sending long fingers into the blue, till the fingers, growing longer and thinner, dissolved and became part of whatever it was they were pointing to.

He blinked again. The sky had moved on.

Great continents now gave birth to islands in some longer process of time than he had been conscious of till now, and the islands too dissolved, like a pill developing fuzzy edges in a glass of water, then diminishing, diminishing. Soon they too had gone. Centuries it must have taken. When he blinked again it was quite a different day or year, or centuries had passed, he couldn't tell which. But he was aware now of the earth he was lying on. It was rolling.

He tried to push himself up on to one elbow so that

he could look about and see where he was. He was conscious of pain, far off over one of the horizons, but couldn't raise himself far enough to locate it. One of the horizons was his own chest. Beyond it a wan light flapped, as if a wounded bird threw faint colours from its wings as its blood beat feebly into the earth. There was nothing he could do about it.

Jim turned his head. Other figures were laid about on all sides of him, some of them groaning, others terribly stilled. He knew he should try to mark his position for the stretcher-bearers, and reached for his rifle which was away to the left; he tried, stretching his fingers, and in a slow access of pain he remembered fingers that had pointed and dissolved, and gazing out over the horizon of his shoulder at his own outstretched fingers, that were still inches from where the rifle lay, saw them too dissolve slowly into the earth, and closed his eyes and let them go. He felt the whole process, a coarsening of the grains out of which his flesh was composed, and their gradual loosening and falling away, as first his hand dissolved, then his arm, then his shoulder. If things went on like this there would be nothing left of him for the bearers to find.

He thought of the emergency field-dressing in the right flap of his tunic. If he worked quickly with his left hand, pulled the tabs and located the little white bag (he had been over all this a hundred times in imagination) he might be able to stop the process of his dissolving, but he would have first to find the place where it had started, the wound; and there was, strangely, not enough pain to give him a clue to where he was hit.

His head? His stomach? He thought of the yards of white bandage – two and a half to be precise – and as before, imagined himself wrapping it round his head. He wrapped and wrapped, the bandage seemed endless. There were thirteen thousand miles of it. It would stretch halfway round the world. To the Coast. To home. He began rolling it, slowly, carefully, in his mind, but before he had gone more than a few inches a feeling of drowsiness crept over him, a slow shadow as of the night, blurring the shape of things. It came over the edge of his body, moved into its hollows, muffled him in silence. He yielded himself up to it.

When he blinked again he was no longer under the sky. There was canvas overhead, and big shadows were moving across it, cast up by an acetylene flare. He was at ground level, far below, and through the open tent-flap came a cooling breeze.

It was crowded in here. But oddly silent. Other fellows, maimed and crudely bandaged, each with a white label tied to a button of his tunic, lay about on all sides, or sat up smoking, very pale and still, leaning together in groups. They had an air of eternal patience, these men; of having given themselves up utterly to a process of slow dissolution like the one he had observed in the sky and felt in his own body. Their eyes had the dumb, apologetic look he had seen in the eyes of horses who had fallen by the roadside and were waiting, without protest, to be shot. Their stillness, their docility, their denseness of flesh and rag and metal, made a sharp contrast with the shadows that moved about the walls of the tent and arched across the roof above them. They swooped and were gigantic. It was on them that the others, patiently, waited: to be touched and attended, to be raised.

Occasionally these shadows took on shape. A white-capped sister, a man in a butcher's apron all sopped with blood. Jim looked and there was a block where the man was working. He could smell it, and the eyes of the others, cowed as they were, took life as they fell upon it.

To his left, on the other side from the men who waited, who were mostly whole, lay the parts of men, the limbs. A jumbled pile.

I am in the wrong place, Jim thought. *I don't belong here. I never asked to be here. I should get going.*

He thought this, but knew that the look on his face must be the same look these other faces wore, anxious, submissive. They were a brotherhood. They had spent their whole life thus, a foot from the block and waiting, even in safe city streets and country yards, even at home in Australia. *Is that it?* Jim wondered. *Is that how it must always be?*

He turned to regard the man on his right, who was also laid out on a palliasse, and saw who it was.

How did he get here?

He closed his eyes. This was the place before the butcher's block. He did not want to be lifted up.

'Jim?'

He knew the voice.

'Jim Saddler?'

He was being called for the second time.

It was Ashley Crowther. He was there, just to the

121

right, also in the shambles. Jim blinked. It was Ashley alright. He was wearing a luggage-label like all the rest, tied with string to one of the buttons of his tunic.

[He had seen Ashley twice since they came to France. Far back in the early days, when things were still quiet, their battalions had been in the same line, and they had stood together one day on a patch of waste-ground, on the same level, just as they might have stood at home, and had a smoke. It was a Sunday afternoon. Cold and still.]

'Listen,' Ashley had said, 'band music.' And Jim, whose ears were keen enough to catch any birdcall but hadn't been aware of the music, heard it blowing faintly towards them from the enemy lines. Had it been there a moment before, or had Ashley somehow conjured it up?

'Von Suppe,' Ashley said, raising a finger to conduct the odd wavering sounds of Sunday afternoon brass.

'Listen' he said now, and his voice came closer. 'Can you hear me, Jim?'

The second occasion had been less than a month ago. They were way to the north, resting, and on the last night, after a whole day's drilling – for rest was just the name of another sort of activity, less dangerous but no less fatiguing than life in the lines – they were marched up the road to an abandoned château where several fellows were sitting about in the late light under trees and others were lining up at a makeshift estaminet.

A piano had been brought down from the château, a

big iron-framed upright with bronze candle-holders. It sat under the trees with a tarpaulin over it in case of rain. Several fellows, one after the other, sang popular songs and they all joined in and a redheaded sergeant from one of the English regiments played a solo on the mouth-organ. Later, a boy whose voice had still to break sang 'O for the wings of a Dove'; it was a sound of such purity, so high, so clear, that the whole orchard was stilled, a voice, neither male nor female, that was, when you lay back and closed your eyes, like the voice of an angel, though when you opened them again and looked, was climbing from the mouth of a child in a patched and ragged uniform no different from the rest, who stood bare-headed in the flickering light from the piano-sconces and when he had finished and unclasped his big hands seemed embarrassed by the emotion he had created, humbled by his own gift.

The concert went on in the dark. Jim heard a nightingale, then another, and tuned his ears, beyond the music, to that – though the music pleased him too; it was good to have both. He thought of Mrs McNamara's contention, so long ago, that it was the most beautiful of all birdsongs, and the other girl's regret that she had never heard it. Well, he had heard it. He was hearing it now. The trees, though they had been badly blasted, were in full leaf, and would in time, even with no one to tend them, bear fruit. It was their nature. Overhead, all upside down as was proper in these parts, were the stars. The guns sounded very far off. It was like summer thunder that you didn't have to concern yourself with: someone else's weather. Jim dozed off.

When he woke it was quite late and the crowd of men had thinned. Someone was playing the piano. Notes, he thought, that might have been taken over from the nightingale's song and elaborated, all tender trills. The strangeness of the place, the open air, or the keying up of his nerves in these last hours before going back, worked strangely upon him and he found himself powerfully affected. He sat up on one elbow and listened.

The music was neither gay nor sad, it didn't need to be either one or the other; it was like the language, beyond known speech, that birds use, which he felt painfully that he might reach out for now and comprehend; and if he did, however briefly, much would become clear to him that would otherwise stay hidden. He looked towards the square wooden frame like an altar with its flickering candles, and immediately recognised the man who was playing. It was Ashley Crowther.

He looked different, changed; Jim was astonished by him. It was as if the music drew him physically together. In the intensity of its occurrence at his finger-ends, his whole body – shoulders, neck, head – came to a kind of attention Jim had not seen there on previous occasions.

Now, still dressed in that new firmness of line, Ashley Crowther was here. His voice once again came close.

'Can you hear me, Jim?'

'Yes.'

He had in the middle of his forehead a small cross. A wound? The mark of Cain? Jim was puzzled. He had seen a man wounded like that, the body quite unmarked and just a small star-shaped hole in the middle of the forehead. Only this was a cross.

'Jim we've got to get out of here. I know the way. Are you strong enough to get up? I'll help you.'

'Yes,' Jim said, deciding to take the risk, and was aware in the darkness of a sudden hiss of breath that was his father's impatience.

He raised himself on his elbows. Ashley leaned down and put a hand under his arm. He was raised, but not towards the block. He stood and Ashley supported him. The relief he felt had something to do with the strength of Ashley's arm – who would ever have expected it? – but also with his own capacity, once more, to accept and trust.

'This way. No one will stop us.'

The nurses were too busy or too tired to observe what they were about, and the man in the bloody apron, all brilliant and deeply shadowed in the light of the flare, was fully engaged at the block. They walked right past them and out under the tent-flap into the night. Jim heaved a great sigh of relief. He too wore a label, its string twisted round one of his tunic buttons. He tore it roughly away now, button and all, and cast it into the mud. He wouldn't need an address label. Though Ashley, he saw, still wore his.

'This way,' Ashley said, and they walked quickly across the field towards a patch of wood. It was clear moonlight.

125

Difficult to say how long they walked. It became light, and off in the woods the birds started up.

'Here,' Ashley said, 'here it is.'

It was a clearing, quite large, and Jim thought he had been here before. And he had, he had! It was the place where he had gone with the others to collect firewood and seen the old man digging. No, not graves, but planting something. He had often thought of the man but the place itself he had forgotten, and he was surprised now to see how thick the woods were, how the blasted trees had renewed themselves with summer growth, covering their wounds, and were turning colour, now that the autumn had come, and stripping. There were thick drifts underfoot. They crackled. A few last birds were singing: two thrushes, and further off somewhere, a chaffinch. Jim moved on out of the softly slanting light. There was a garden in the clearing, neat rows of what looked like potatoes, and figures, dark-backed and slowly moving, were on their knees between the plants, digging.

He freed himself of Ashley's support, and staggered towards them. The earth smelled so good. It was a smell that belonged to the beginning of things, he could have put his nose down into it like a pig or a newly weaned calf, and the thought of filling his hands with its doughy softness was irresistible. To have dirt under his nails! Falling on his knees he began awkwardly to knead the earth, which was warm, damp, delightfully crumbly, and then to claw at it as the others were doing. It felt good.

'That's it, mate. That's the style! Dig!'

126

Jim looked around, astonished. It was Clancy Parkett, whom he had last seen nearly a year ago, and
whom he believed was dead, blown into so many
pieces that nothing of him was ever found except what
Jim himself had been covered with. To give poor
Clancy a decent burial, some wit had said, they would
have had to bury the both of them. And now here he
was quite whole after all, grinning and rasping his
chin with a blackened thumb. Trust Clancy. Clancy
would wriggle out of anything.

'I thought you'd been blown up,' Jim said foolishly.
'You just disappeared into thin air.'

'No,' Clancy told him, 'not air, mate. Earth.' And he
held up a fistful of the richly smelling mud. 'It's the
only way now. We're digging through to the other
side.'

'But it'll take so long,' Jim said reasonably.

Clancy laughed. 'There's all the time in the world,
mate. No trouble about time. And it's better than tryin'
t' walk it.'

Jim, doubtful, began to dig. He looked about.
Others were doing the same, long lines of them, and
he was surprised to see how large the clearing was. It
stretched away to the brightening skyline. It wasn't a
clearing but a field, and more than a field, a landscape;
so wide, as the early morning sun struck the furrows,
that you could see the curve of the earth. There were
hundreds of men, all caked with mud, long-haired,
bearded, in ragged uniforms, stooped to the black
earth and digging. So it must be alright after all. Why
else should so many be doing it? The lines stretched

out forever. He could hardly make out the last men, they were so small in the distance. And Clancy. Clancy was no fool.

He began to dig in earnest. He looked about once, seeking Ashley, but Ashley Crowther was no longer in sight.

So Jim dug along with the rest. The earth was rich and warm, it smelled of all that was good, and his back did not ache as he had expected. Nor did his knees. And there was, after all, time, however far it might be. The direct route – straight through. He looked up, meeting Clancy's humorous gaze, and they both grinned. It might be, Jim thought, what hands were intended for, this steady digging into the earth, as wings were meant for flying over the curve of the planet to another season. He knelt and dug.

18

Imogen Harcourt, still carrying her equipment – camera, plates, tripod – as she had once told Jim, 'like the implements of martyrdom,' made her way down the soft sand of the dunes towards the beach.

A clear October day.

October here was spring. Sunlight and no wind.

The sea cut channels in the beach, great Vs that were delicately ridged at the edges and ribbed within, and the sunlit rippled in them, an inch, an inch and a half of shimmering gold. Further on, the surf. High walls of water were suspended a moment, held glassily aloft, then hurled themselves forward under a shower of spindrift, a white rush that ran hissing to her boots. There were gulls, dense clouds of them hanging low over the white-caps, feeding, oystercatchers darting after crabs, crested terns. A still scene that was full of intense activity and endless change.

She set down her equipment – she didn't intend to do any work; she carried all this stuff by force of habit and because she didn't like to be separated from it, it was all she had, an extension of herself that couldn't now be relinquished. She eased the strap off her shoulder, set it all down and then sat dumpily beside it, a lone figure with her hat awry, on the white sands that stretched as far as the eye could see, all the way to the Broadwater and the southern tip of Stradbroke in one direction and in the other to Point Danger and the New South Wales border. It was all untouched. Nobody came here. Before her, where she sat with her boots dug in and her knees drawn up, was the Pacific, blue to the skyline, and beyond it, Peru.

'What am I doing here?' she asked herself, putting the question for maybe the thousandth time and finding no answer, but knowing that if she were back in Norfolk there would be the same question to be put and with no answer there either.

'I am doing' she told herself firmly, 'what those gulls are doing. Those oystercatchers. Those terns.' She pulled her old hat down hard on her curls.

The news of Jim's death had already arrived. She heard it by accident in the local store, then she heard it again from Julia Crowther, with the news that Ashley Crowther had been wounded in the same battle, though not in the same part of the field, and was convalescing in England. Then one day she ran into Jim's father.

'I lost my boy,' he told her accusingly. He had never addressed her before.

'I know,' she said. 'I'm very sorry.'

He regarded her fiercely. She had wanted to say more, to say that she understood a little of what he might feel, that for two whole days after she heard she

130

had been unable to move; but that would have been to boast of her grief and claim for herself something she had no right to and which was too personal to be shared, though she felt, obscurely, that to share it with this man who was glaring at her so balefully and with such a deep hatred for everything he saw, might be to offer him some release from himself and to let Jim, now that he was dead, back into his life. What did he feel? What was his grief like? She couldn't tell, any more than he could have guessed at or measured hers. She said nothing. He didn't invite sympathy. It wasn't for that that he had approached her.

She sat on the beach now and watched the waves, one after another, as they rose, gathered themselves, stood poised a moment holding the sun at their crests, then toppled. There was a rhythm to it. Mathematics. It soothed, it allowed you, once you had perceived it, to breathe. Maybe she would go on from birds to waves. They were as various and as difficult to catch at their one moment.

That was it, the thought she had been reaching for. Her mind gathered and held it, on a breath, before the pull of the earth drew it apart and sent it rushing down with such energy into the flux of things. What had torn at her breast in the fact of Jim's death had been the waste of it, all those days that had been gathered towards nothing but his senseless and brutal extinction. Her pain lay in the acute vision she had had of his sitting as she had seen him on that first day, all his intense being concentrated on the picture she had taken of the sandpiper, holding it tight in his hand, but

131

holding it also in his eye, his mind, absorbed in the uniqueness of the small creature as the camera had caught it at just that moment, with its head cocked and its fierce alert eye, and in entering that one moment of the bird's life – the bird was gone, they might never see it again – bringing up to the moment, in her vision of him, his own being that was just then so very like the birds, alert, unique, utterly present. ⌉

It was that intense focus of his whole being, it's *me*, Jim Saddler, that struck her with grief, but was also the thing – and not simply as an image either – that endured. That in itself. Not as she might have preserved it in a shot she had never in fact taken, nor even as she had held it, for so long, as an untaken image in her head, but in itself, as it for its moment was. That is what life meant, a unique presence, and it was essential in every creature. To set anything above it, birth, position, talent even, was to deny to all but a few among the infinite millions what was common and real, and what was also, in the end, most moving. A life wasn't *for* anything. It simply was.

She watched the waves build, hang and fall, one after the other in decades, in centuries, all morning and on into the early afternoon; and was preparing, wearily, to gather up her equipment and start back – had risen in fact, and shouldered the tripod, when she saw something amazing.

A youth was walking – no, running, on the water. Moving fast over the surface. Hanging delicately balanced there with his arms raised and his knees slightly bent as if upheld by invisible strings. She had seen nothing like it. He rode rapidly towards her; then, on the crest of the wave, sharply outlined against the sky, went down fast into the darkening hollow, fell, and she saw a kind of plank flash in the sunlight and go flying up behind him.

She stood there. Fascinated. The youth, retrieving the board among the flurry of white in the shallows, knelt upon it and began paddling out against the waves. Far out, a mere dot on the sunlit water, where the waves gathered and began, she saw him paddle again, then miraculously rise, moving faster now, and the whole performance was repeated: the balance, the still dancing on the surface, the brief etching of his body against the sky at the very moment, on the wave's lip, when he would slide into its hollows and fall.

That too was an image she would hold in her mind.

Jim, she said to herself, *Jim, Jim*, and hugged her breast a little, raising her face to the light breeze that had come with afternoon, feeling it cold where the tears ran down. The youth, riding towards her, was blurred in the moment before the fall.

She took up her camera and set the strap to her shoulder. There was a groove. She turned her back to the sea and began climbing the heavy slope, where her boots sank and filled and the grains rolled away softly behind. At the top, among the pigweed that held the dunes together, she turned, and the youth was still there, his arms extended, riding.

It was new. So many things were new. Everything changed. The past would not hold and could not be

133

held. One day soon, she might make a photograph of this new thing. To catch its moment, its brilliant balance up there, of movement and stillness, of tense energy and ease – that would be something.

This eager turning, for a moment, to the future, surprised and hurt her.

Jim, she moaned silently, somewhere deep inside. *Jim. Jim*. There was in there a mourning woman who rocked eternally back and forth; who would not be seen and was herself.

But before she fell below the crest of the dunes, while the ocean was still in view, she turned and looked again.